# Sea Glass Memories

Seahaven Sunrise Book 2

Anne Marie Bennett

***Sea Glass Memories*** is a work of fiction. Names, characters, businesses, places, events, locales, and incidents are either the products of the author's imagination or used in a fictitious manner. Any resemblance to actual persons, living or dead, or actual Events, is purely coincidental.





Published in the United States by KaleidoSoul Media
PO Box 745, Beverly MA 01915
AnneMarieBennett.com

Book design by Kozakura on Fiverr.com
Cover design by Lynn Andreozzi

Images on cover from borojoint on DepositPhotos.com
and boulham on shutterstock.com

Print ISBN: 979-8-9860503-4-8
Digital ISBN: 979-8-9860503-5-5

# Sea Glass Memories

Seahaven Sunrise Book 2

# Dedication

*For those who know firsthand*
*that grief is the price we pay for loving.*

*May you honor and tend to*
*the bruised space in your heart*
*that holds the memories*
*of those you feel but cannot see.*

*Those whom we love do indeed leave us,*
*and when we lose them no spoken words can lessen our grief.*
*But what they were can never leave us.*

*The strength of their presence,*
*the gentleness of their sympathy,*
*the warmth of their love-*
*these are ours always,*
*interfused with our thought and blended with our lives.*

**~ A. Powell Davies**

# Chapter 1

## ELENA JEFFRIES

*There's an old* cartoon where someone is huddled under a heap of blankets and doesn't want to get out of bed because it's the first day of school. An adult comes along and throws the covers off, saying, "You need to go to school today, sweetie. You're the *teacher*."

Well, today I'm the teacher—the new English teacher at Seahaven High—and the joke isn't funny, mainly because there's no one here to throw the covers off me. Mom and Dad are gone, and so is Marc. Part of me does not want to get out of bed today. Everything feels so new and strange. Just last week I packed up our … I mean my … little house in Dorchester and moved up here to Maine for this job. Okay, I'll be honest. I didn't move here only for the job. The biggest reason for this change was to start over somewhere new, a place with no traces of Marc or my other life.

No, I don't want to get out of bed. Everything about this first day of school is hard. But I do what I must do—I throw back the covers and sit on the edge of the bed for a minute, trying to get my bearings. Jezebel, my spunky black cat with the surprisingly white whiskers, stretches and yawns from her comfy spot nearby, then nuzzles her face against my shoulder. I sigh and kiss the top of her head.

I'm not a stranger to first days of school as a teacher. This will be my eighth, but the other seven were spent in the Boston Public School system at Dorchester High. I used to look forward to the first day of school. I love turning teenagers on to reading and writing. Back then, Marc was always there to wake me up with kisses and coffee in bed before he went off to work at Fidelity Investments. For the last two years, however, I've had to depend on my phone alarm because Marc is completely and utterly gone, the casualty of a fatal car accident one November afternoon. I was at a doctor's appointment that day and I deeply regret that I wasn't with him in the car, but not for the reason you might be thinking. There was something I didn't get to tell Marc before he died and that is what I regret the most.

I get out of bed slowly. My body hasn't felt the same since he died, but I stretch anyway and head to the shower. A few boxes of Marc's things sit in the corner of my bedroom. My *new* bedroom. Everything still looks strange, unfamiliar. I hate looking at those boxes, but the closet isn't big enough and I don't know where else to put them.

As I splash cold water on my face, I gaze at myself in the mirror and frown. I don't have time to wash my hair—it's long, black, and thick—so I gather it into a tight ponytail and stuff it all under a voluminous shower cap. I blink at myself and try to smile, but my eyes appear tired, my face looks pale. It's hard, starting at a new school. I was there for orientation on Friday, and I have to say, Seahaven High is a whole world away from Dorchester. For one thing, there's more money in the town's school budget. More books, more resources, more computers. And the teachers here? They look brighter, happier, less exhausted. Maybe that's because it's only the start of the school year, but I don't think so. It could be the fresh sea air. I don't know. Maybe this change of scenery will make me brighter, happier, and less exhausted too. If I can make it until June.

Before I can step into the shower, my phone rings. It's my big brother, Carlos. I reassure him that I'm awake. Carlos is five years older than me. He moved to Maine the year after Dad died, got a degree in nearby York as a veterinary assistant, and now works at Bright Side Animal Clinic with Dr. Brightman here in Seahaven. Carlos has always loved animals, so we weren't surprised when he made this change. I was thirteen, and when he left, it was just me and Mom. She died my first year of college, so now it's just me and Carlos. I am so grateful for him. He was there for me when Mom died, and when Marc died too. I don't know what my life would be like without him.

Carlos is the real reason I'm here—in Maine—instead of Massachusetts. After Marc died, *I* wanted to die, and I'll be the first to admit that Carlos is also the reason why I'm actually still *here*—not in Maine, but on this *planet*—alive and breathing. He's the only one I let close to me during those dark, difficult months of living with such unexpected, searing grief. He took extra time off from the clinic to stay with me. My big brother. He kept me tethered to this planet when I so desperately wanted to leave.

His new boyfriend, Jasper, lives in one of the four apartments in this renovated Victorian which is owned by an older woman, Kit Gilmore. She used to be a well-known model in New York. According to Carlos, she was waiting for the right person to show up to rent it. They all seemed to think that I was that person. I had my doubts, but when Carlos also told me there was an opening at Seahaven High for an English teacher, I let myself be convinced.

*A change of scenery would be good for you*, he had said.

At this point, I figure I've got nothing left to lose.

Only time will tell if he was right.

On my way into school, I check in at the front office. It's so early that the office workers aren't even here yet. I've always been someone who likes to be uber-early, but today there's another reason for getting here before everyone else—I just want to get to my classroom and look over my lesson plans one more time. I intend to be an island unto myself today, so I can do what I do best—teach. I feel like I'm on "new people" overload after meeting a lot of the staff members at Friday's teacher orientation. On Sunday night, Jasper invited Carlos and everyone in the apartments to this weird (but strangely interesting) "backwards dinner."

Don't get me wrong. I liked meeting Tess and her eleven-year-old daughter Eva, along with Glory and her grandkids Kalila and Samuel. I have to admit, I enjoyed the silliness of wearing my shirt backwards and even laughed a bit to see how carried away a few of the others got with the theme. It was nice to get to know Jasper because Carlos is head over heels in love with him. Tess's boyfriend, Luca, was also there, along with Kit whom everyone called "Aunt Kit" even though she's only related to Tess and Eva. Yes, everyone at the backwards dinner and teacher orientation was warm and welcoming, but frankly, I found it exhausting.

I wasn't always this way—an island unto myself. Marc used to say that I was the life of the party. In his wedding vows, he mentioned my "sparkling personality and ability to make anyone and everyone feel at home." I guess I *was* like that—outgoing, a people person. I was like that *before*. Now? I keep to myself. I teach. I go home. I read, correct papers, make my supper, play with Jezebel, and try to sleep. I wake up to the alarm instead of kisses and coffee. Fast forward through another day. And … Repeat. It's so much easier this way. Definitely lonelier, but somewhat easier.

As I'm taking several announcement pages out of my new mailbox—**ELENA JEFFRIES** in bold letters taped to the bottom—a man enters the office and stands beside me. I am tall but he is taller. I notice a pleasant enough face that shows off hazel eyes rimmed with gold, partially obscured by a pair of tortoise shell eyeglasses. Our hands collide as his mailbox is directly next to mine, and I look away quickly. "Another early bird, I see!" he quips, tucking a folder and some loose papers under his left arm. He sets down a well-worn briefcase and offers me his right hand.

I was hoping to escape into my classroom without having to talk to anyone, but I take his hand and feel the comfort of human touch, something that's been sorely lacking in my life since Marc died. Jezebel is soft and warm, but that's not the kind of comfort I'm referring to. "I like to get a head start on the day," I mumble.

"Me too," he replies amenably. "You're the new English teacher, right?" He stuffs the announcement sheets into the outside pocket of his briefcase and looks at me expectantly, his eyes intense but cheerful.

"Yes, Elena Jeffries." A few friends had suggested I take back my maiden name, Fuentes, but I couldn't do that. I'll never do that. I took Marc's name when I married him and I don't want to let it go. It's the last thing I have left of him, the last thing that was ours and ours alone. Well, almost the last thing.

"Glad to meet you. I'm Jonathan MacKenna, U.S. History teacher and Senior Class Adviser. I didn't get a chance to talk with you at orientation."

"Right. There were so many people and I still don't have everyone's names straight." I clutch the papers from the mailbox, hoisting the large Laurel Burch tote bag onto my shoulder. It's printed with one of her signature colorful cat designs that always lifts my spirits. "It's nice to meet you. I need to get to my classroom now." Head down, I move toward the door for the hallway, express getaway in sight.

"Let me know if you need anything," he calls after me, but I am already out the door and up the stairs.

All in all, it's a pretty good first day. I am teaching one class of Freshman English, two classes of sophomore American Literature and two classes of Creative Writing which is mostly seniors. The kids, for the most part, seem eager to please. As usual, I still need to watch out for a few in each class who are on either end of the personality spectrum—either too bashful to speak up, or too eager to monopolize the conversation. Always a challenge for any teacher, new or experienced.

Even though I try to give all my students the benefit of the doubt at the beginning—not reading reports from former teachers until the second week—there are usually a few who stand out to me right away. Today there are three: Kalila Jones, Benjamin Cho, and Maggie Bessima. All three are seniors, and all are in my last period Creative Writing class.

I avoid the teacher's lounge by staying in my classroom and eating lunch at my desk. The turkey salad wrap that I brought from home tastes especially good at my break because I didn't have time to eat breakfast. That's what I get for needing to be here so early.

On my way to the parking lot at the end of the day, I run into Jonathan again. He grins and offers me a sharp but playful salute. "How was your first day, Mrs. Jeffries?"

I stop and shift the heavy tote bag to my other shoulder, eager to go through the students' essays. Remember how your teachers asked you to write about *What I Did on My Summer Vacation*? Boring! I like to assign a different topic: *What I Wish I'd Done on My Summer Vacation.* I learn a lot more about my students this way.

"Not too bad," I reply. "But it's actually *Miss* … I mean, *Ms. Jeffries."*

"Oh … " He hesitates. "Sorry, I thought you were married." He glances at my left hand. Yes, I'm still wearing my wedding ring. Sue me.

"I am … You see, I was married but—"

Jonathan nods. "I get it. He left you but you're still hoping to get back together."

"What?" I stop gazing longingly at my car and lift my eyes to meet his. "No, that's not it at all." This conversation never gets easier. It would be helpful if I'd stop wearing my wedding ring but I can't seem to let it go. "My husband died almost two years ago, which means I'm not really a Mrs. anymore. Although I like it when the kids call me that." I see his cheeks flush with embarrassment and feel a bit sorry for him.

"Open mouth, insert foot." He plunks his briefcase down and places both hands on top of his head. "I'm sorry. For your loss, of course, and also for being an idiot." He looks positively mortified.

"It's okay," I say, somehow touched by this display of emotion. It takes a good man to apologize, I've always thought. "Not your fault. Let's dispense with the formalities. Call me Elena."

Jonathan lets out a breath and smiles again. Funny, but it seems like the sky lightens when he smiles at me. I glance up at the sky but it's the same September-blue that it was five minutes ago.

"Elena it is. Hey, want to head over to Simply Sweets with me now? We can share a dish of ice cream and talk smack about our students."

I raise my eyebrows.

"I'm kidding. About the kids, not the ice cream. Hey, you like ice cream, don't you?"

"Um … "

"And while we're there I can tell you my own sad story. I mean, you told me yours, so I could tell you mine. Believe me, it's a whopper."

The tote bag is feeling extra heavy right now so I walk a few steps to my car and open the back door so I can set the bag down. Jonathan is still standing where I left him. Waiting. Expectantly. I turn to him and say, "I can't go for ice cream because I promised Kit Gilmore … Do you know her?"

He nods. "Sure do. Everyone here knows Aunt Kit. She's not my aunt, obviously, but everyone loves her so that's what we call her. How do you know her?"

"She owns the apartment building I'm living in, over on Bright Blessing Way. Anyway, she invited me to a grief support group meeting this afternoon at the Community Center. I think it's called *Together Not Alone*. I promised to meet her there at four o'clock. But thanks for the invitation." He studies me for a moment, perhaps trying to evaluate if I'm being sincere or if I'm blowing him off. But who would use a grief support group as an excuse? Definitely not me. Although, if I didn't have this very real explanation, I wonder if I would have gone with him. I do love ice cream. And he seems like a very nice guy.

"Yes, I know about the group. My aunt goes there sometimes. Okay, maybe another time?"

I note the hopefulness in his voice but all I can say is, "Maybe." We get into our cars—which just happen to be parked next to each other—and go our separate ways.

# *Chapter 2*

*I find the* Seahaven Community Center easily enough; it's a few miles from the high school, close to downtown. When I finally find the right meeting room, several people are standing around a long table, pouring coffee, and snacking on what looks like homemade chocolate chip cookies. Kit waves at me from across the meeting space and beckons me over. She's wearing one of those serene outfits that I already associate with her—billowy white pants and a flowy teal top that sets off her long silvery hair and kind, gray eyes. "Elena, you made it! How was your first day?" She hugs me as if we hadn't just met when I moved into her apartment building. At first I stiffen, but then something inside of me starts to soften. My brother Carlos is the only one who has hugged me in a very long time. Besides Jezebel, but that's not the kind of hug I'm referring to.

"It was good," I reply, noting the laugh lines that fan out from her eyes. Otherwise, Kit's skin is remarkably smooth and supple for someone in her sixties. I search for some words to reassure her that she did the right thing by renting me the apartment. "I'm glad I came to Seahaven." As soon as the words come out of my mouth, I'm surprised to realize they're true.

"That is the best news I've heard all day, dear!" She puts her arm around me and guides me to a woman holding a clipboard and a green pen. “Elena, this is Leah St. James: Social Worker Extraordinaire, and leader of our support group. Leah, this is Elena Jeffries, the new English teacher at SHS.”

Leah appears to be several years younger than Kit. She has dark eyes and short auburn hair lightly threaded with gray. Leah smiles warmly and offers her hand in what feels like a genuine welcome. “Elena, I’m so glad you’re here! Why don’t you two have a seat, and I’ll gather everyone so we can get started.”

I have to say, when Kit first told me about this group—*Together Not Alone*—last week at Jasper’s backwards dinner, I was taken aback. Carlos had told me that Kit’s fiancé died when they were both twenty years old, which was more than forty years ago. She couldn’t possibly *still* need a support group to help her through her grief, could she? And if so, what does that mean for me? Thirty years from now, when my hair has turned gray, will I still be needing therapy to get through this dreadful ache I feel whenever I think of Marc? I sure hope not. I know I’ll never forget him. He was my whole life and I loved him with all my heart. And yet. I really want this loneliness to be gone.

I sigh as I glance at Kit. She’s talking quietly with the older woman on her right. I didn’t want to come to this meeting but I had a long talk with Camille—my therapist from Boston—and she convinced me that it was time to branch out from one-on-one therapy with her. So here I am. Curious, but unconvinced. Besides, it gave me a good excuse to turn down Jonathan’s invitation. Yes, I’m lonely, but I’m not quite sure I’m ready to let someone else in right now.

Leah is wearing a knee-length pale blue linen shift dress and a navy tailored jacket. The white tennis shoes and cuffed socks on her feet are seemingly at odds with her professional attire. She settles herself into a folding chair across from us as several others silently fill in the remaining seats. For the first time, I notice there is a small round table in the center of our circle of chairs. It's covered with a plain white cloth that flows gracefully to the floor. Atop the table is a shallow glass bowl filled with pieces of sea glass—all sizes, shapes, and colors. It captures my attention. I sense that it is meaningful but wonder what it has to do with a grief support group. Camille urged me to keep an open mind, so I allow my curiosity to hold me in my seat.

"Welcome to TNA." Leah's hands rest lightly on her thighs. She looks completely relaxed and at home as she looks around at the circle of faces. There are no rings on her fingers or bracelets on her wrists, although she is wearing a pair of small hoop earrings and a delicate silver starfish charm on a chain around her neck. "This is Seahaven's support group for those who are grieving any kind of loss. My name is Leah St. James and I'm a licensed clinical social worker from Seahaven Child and Family Services. Let's take a few minutes to go around the circle so everyone can introduce themselves. Tell us your first name and what kind of loss you're experiencing. Feel free to pass; it's okay to simply listen today if that's what you need. Let me remind you all that this is a safe place, and we don't share anything heard in this room … outside of this room. We keep the group sharing confidential, right *here*." At this, Leah places her right hand over her heart and makes eye contact with each person. When she meets my gaze, I nod slightly and look away. Her kindness is overwhelming. I wonder what grief she is bearing and if it is similar to my own.

Leah continues. "Okay. I will begin. My name is Leah and I lost my husband to divorce last year, right after losing my left breast to cancer. Also, my cat, Buddy, who has been my lifeline through it all, is sick. He's on medication and it's working for now, but I don't know how much time he has left."

I swallow hard when I hear this. Her losses are nothing like mine, but they are monumental and terrible, all the same. I shift in my seat and join in as the others murmur, "Welcome, Leah."

Next to me, Kit raises her hand slightly. "I'll go next. I'm Kit and my biggest loss was long ago. My fiancé died when we were twenty. Ollie had a rare, undetected heart defect and died in his sleep. But I'm here today because a few weeks ago, Ollie's mother died. Lillian had pancreatic cancer and it was mercifully quick. She was more like a mother to me than my own mother was, so … " I notice tears in her eyes and reach over to squeeze her hand. "Thanks for listening."

"Welcome, Kit."

I listen carefully as the others introduce themselves and their losses. Having spent so much time over the last year and a half in therapy with Camille, I'm no stranger to talking about grief. Camille is even older than Kit, and much wiser than I'll probably ever be. She mostly listened to me during our sessions, but when she spoke, she did so from a wider perspective that always gave me comfort and hope.

Of all the people here, Kit's loss is the most recent. A few have lost a parent, and there are some widowers and divorced folks too. I am listening now to a much older woman who has short spiky hair the color of pale tiger lilies. It looks like she's bouncing in her seat, reminding me of a hyperactive student in one of my classes today (but he was fifteen and she must be at least five times that). "Hello everyone. You already know me but there's a newcomer, so I'll say more. I'm Bea Lively." She breaks into the silliest giggle I've ever heard from an adult.

I've never heard a grandmotherly type of woman giggle before, but I have to admit—I like it!

"Be Lively … get it?" She's looking right at me so I give her a thumbs up. "That's me! Lively as all get out. Isn't it great that my parents named me Beatrice? They had no idea—"

Leah clears her throat. "Bea! Let's get back on track."

"Right-o! Apologies to all! As the kids today say, *my bad.*"

Leah grins and motions for Bea to continue.

"Anywho, I'm here because my brother died earlier this year and we weren't close, so that's like two losses in one." She clasps her hands to her chest and squeezes her eyes shut, then whispers, "Thanks for listening."

After the now-familiar welcome chant, Aunt Kit nudges me gently. "It's your turn now, if you want to share."

I feel my face heat up. The others are looking at me curiously. You might think this wouldn't be uncomfortable because I face several groups of expectant faces every day at school. But it is. It is very different. "Sure. I'm Elena. I moved here last week to teach English at Seahaven High. My husband died … It will be two years in November." I pause. Do they want to know more? How much should I share? Do I tell them the worst part of it all? No, I'm not ready for that. "It was a freak car accident. His name was Marc."

"Welcome, Elena." I can feel the group's attention and presence and it lifts me somehow. Maybe Camille was right. Maybe there is another dimension to sharing my grief in a group like this.

As Leah leads us in a breathing exercise, I feel my shoulders relaxing a bit more. Looking around the group as we slow our breathing, I notice that, somehow, everyone looks familiar to me already.

"Now … " Leah takes one final deep breath through her nose and lets it out slowly through her mouth. "I'm glad you're all here, each and every one of you, especially our newcomer, Elena. It takes a lot of courage to step into a group like this and I want to acknowledge that."

I smile and feel her warmth reaching a tender place inside me. I have never considered myself courageous, so that's something new to think about.

Leah continues. "We'll finish up right at five-thirty, so please be time conscious if you choose to share. If you have anything you need to get off your mind or heart, please take a piece of sea glass from the bowl before you begin. You can choose to keep it when you leave or put it back. I have plenty more at home, not to worry!"

Everyone chuckles but I am fixated on the bowl of many colors. I raise my hand tentatively. "Is there a story about the sea glass? It seems to be important, but I don't know why."

Leah begins to speak, but a woman about her age quickly stands up. Even though she's wearing jeans and a fuchsia sleeveless top, she appears professional and at ease; her white-blonde hair falls to her shoulders gracefully in a blunt cut. "I'll explain, Leah, if you don't mind."

"Go right ahead, Anna."

Anna takes two pieces of sea glass from the bowl, hands an aqua one to me, then takes her seat and holds a grass-green one up to the florescent ceiling lights. Her fingernails glow rose-gold against the glass. "I'm so grateful for this group. My husband died suddenly of a heart attack several months ago. Six months and five days, to be exact." She squeezes her eyes shut for a few seconds and takes a deep breath. "Now, about the sea glass. Leah has been collecting it for years, long before the cancer diagnosis. Before her jerk of a husband left her."

Leah nods slowly and the rest of the group murmurs agreement. I can tell they've heard this story more than once.

"Elena, trace your fingers around the edge of the piece you're holding. How does it feel?"

"Smooth," I reply immediately, enjoying the sensation of the flat, cool glass against my skin.

"You're right. The edges are smooth. They got that way from years of the ocean's waves and sand washing over them. What you're holding started out as a piece of broken glass, maybe from a bottle or jar of some kind. When glass breaks, the edges are jagged and sharp. They can be used as weapons … "

"They can wound us," Leah prompts gently.

"Yes, we need to be careful with pieces of broken glass, just like we have to be careful with our grief. But with time and the roughness of the ocean, the sharp edges of fragmented glass become smoother."

"Like us?" I interrupt.

"That's right," Leah takes a piece of clear sea glass from the bowl as Anna sits down. "When we experience grief, instead of feeling whole, it can feel as if we've been broken into pieces that are tumbling around inside us like shards of glass in the ocean. The sea glass helps us remember that the pain of any kind of loss—any kind of brokenness—has the potential to soften if we allow ourselves to be with it. Our tears, our rage, our denial, our anguish—over time—can smooth the rough edges of our grief. I also believe that we can hold onto the sea glass as a reminder of what we have lost as well as how we survived it."

The group is silent as I try to absorb her words. "Are you saying that the pain is never going to go away? I mean, there are lots of days now when Marc only crosses my mind a few times. And it hurts a lot less than it did two years ago, but … " I'm clenching the aqua glass in my fist so tightly that my palms are beginning to sweat. "I don't want the hurting to go away forever because I think it means I'll forget him." My fingers slowly unfold of their own accord and I look to Leah for a response.

"I haven't lost a husband or partner to death, so I think there might be others here who are better qualified to answer that. Anna? Kit? Chelsea?"

Anna smiles at me; I have the feeling she knows where I'm coming from. "I'm a few months away from the worst of the pain," she says. "For me, it's not like the pain actually goes away. It's more like I'm growing a bigger space inside me so I can carry all of it more easily—the sorrow, along with the good memories. Does that make sense?"

My forehead wrinkles in concentration. "I'm going to have to think about this for a while."

Kit pats my hand; her touch is soothing. "Take all the time you need. My Ollie is still with me here … " She taps her heart lightly. "… and the memories we shared cause me to smile now instead of weep."

"Yes," adds Chelsea, a woman about my age wearing jean shorts and a bright red batik top. My husband died four years ago and I can honestly say that after a few years, what the others are saying is true. But you have to allow the tears and the anger … and whatever else you may be feeling … to be the waves that soften the edges of the sorrow. After that, the memories become much clearer and easier to remember."

I swallow hard. All these people. All these difficult losses. "Do you remember how you felt after two years?"

Bea taps two fingers against her lips and smiles kindly. "Everyone is different, honey. Keep the focus on your own journey, however it progresses. It takes as long as it takes."

"Is there some reason why you're asking about the two-year mark?" Leah asks.

"Well, November eleventh is the two-year anniversary of his death," I reply nervously, looking around the circle. There is something extraordinary about being seen and heard like this. No one is judging me or trying to change my grief like I thought they might. "I'm starting to wonder if I'm going to be alone for the rest of my life. I mean, I don't want to replace Marc or anything, but … " My voice trails off. I've surprised myself by saying this out loud; I've hardly even admitted this to myself.

"Oh, I understand," Chelsea replies. She has gorgeous blond

hair, swept back in a colorful scarf that matches her top. "It's a different kind of loneliness that you're experiencing now. You're not quite ready to let go of Marc, but you're wondering if there might be someone else out there for you."

I feel both validated and relieved. "Yes. Exactly."

Bea lifts her hands in the air as if she's about to conduct an orchestra and says brightly, "Sweetie, maybe it's time to start dating again. I don't know … " She slaps her hands onto her knees. "What do the kids say today? Play the field a bit? Get your toes wet?"

I smile at her enthusiasm. Maybe she's right. That teacher at school today—Jonathan—invited me for ice cream and I was relieved to have an excuse. "I guess I have a lot to think about," I reply. "Thank you everyone. I'm glad to be here."

For the rest of the meeting, I listen carefully as men, women, and one teenager share their stories. Each person takes a piece of sea glass as they talk. A few times we pass around a box of tissues. Their stories are no easier or harder than mine; the stories are different, but the feelings are the same. It is difficult being in a room where so much sadness is being expressed, yet it feels good somehow because our words of grief are being witnessed. Within the space of that witnessing, tiny pieces of sorrow are lifted. In that lifting, there is hope.

After the meeting, Bea rushes up to me, hands outstretched. "Darling girl," she says with a grin so wide I'm afraid it will hurt her face. "I'm pleased as punch that you joined us today and I hope you'll come back again and again."

"Thanks, I—"

"Now. I know you're new here and all, but I want you to know that Seahaven is the friendliest place on Earth. You might think that it's Disneyland, but no! It's us! Right here in lil' ol' small-town Maine. Have you seen a sunrise here yet?" She doesn't even pause to take a breath or notice that I'm shaking my head. "These are the best sunrises you will ever see, although I do hear the ones in South Africa are quite breathtaking. Anywho, listen." She pats my arm with her surprisingly strong plump hand. "I want to invite you to the dress rehearsal for *Into the Woods* at Sands of Time Theatre. Thursday night. Some of the others from TNA are also coming. I'm the House Manager which means I'm in charge of all the ushers and making sure everyone is seated on time, and because I'm staff, I can invite whoever I want to the dress rehearsal."

I pause to take a breath even though Bea doesn't seem to have the same need. Her lung capacity appears to be perfectly fine.

"So! Will you come? I hope you'll come, dear!" Bea clasps her hands to her chest and for a moment, I can see the lively little girl that she used to be.

I pause to see if she has stopped her flighty chatter. It appears that she has; hope flashes from her vivid blue eyes and her smile is contagious. "I'll see how much I have to do after school that day, but I'll try." The thought of seeing a live show again sends a startling thrill through my body. It's been over two years since I sat in a darkened theatre and that was to see *Camelot* with Marc at the Shubert in Boston.

I'm wondering what it will be like to enter a theatre without Marc by my side when Bea interrupts my anxious thoughts. "Don't forget! Thursday night. Seven p.m. Come in the main entrance and look for me! There's someone I want you meet after the rehearsal." She winks, blows me a kiss, and turns away to grab hold of Leah who is heading for the door.

# Chapter 3

*As many times* as I try to talk myself out of going to the *Into the Woods* dress rehearsal, I find myself looking forward to it. It's not a show I'm familiar with but I think it has something to do with an array of miscellaneous fairy tales that are strung together into one story.

I asked Kit to go with me but she's working at her shop downtown—Coastal Soul—where she sells all kinds of unique gifts, jewelry, and books. I've been so busy that I haven't had time yet to check it out. She also teaches classes on mindfulness and intuition but that's too "out there" for me. Don't get me wrong, I've only known her a short time, but I already love Kit. She was warm and welcoming before I'd even met her, and she doesn't seem like the type to force her beliefs on others. When I do visit her shop, chances are good that I will buy something, but I'll leave the classes to someone else.

My brother Carlos loves theatre but he's also at work since Bright Side Animal Clinic is open on Thursday nights. His boyfriend Jasper, who lives in my apartment building and does maintenance work for Kit, will be at the dress rehearsal because he is also the props master at Sands of Time.

There's no one at school that I know well enough to ask yet, so I guess I'm going alone. I shrug into a light sweater over my favorite silk tank top and jeans, smooth my long hair back into a loose ponytail, and try to calm the nerves that are fizzing in my stomach. Here goes nothing.

On second thought, this is a pretty big step for me. So, maybe … here goes everything?

Bea finds me as soon as I walk into the semi-dark theatre. “Elena!” She’s standing a few rows from the stage and shouts my name so loudly and gestures so wildly that others who are already seated turn around to look at me. “Come on down!” Her voice is clear and strong; I am warmed inside and out by her welcome. She wears black pants, a white shirt and royal purple vest with the theatre logo and a name badge on her left lapel. Cherry-red half-glasses tilt down on her nose, and her tiger-lily hair is short and spiky.

As I approach the first few rows, I also see the welcoming smiles of Leah, Anna, and a few others from TNA. My breath steadies as I realize that I am not among strangers. Bea introduces me to several ushers wearing a similar uniform, and tells me that they’d love to add me to their volunteer list. As usual, I am made a little unsteady by Bea’s just-short-of-manic rush of energy, so I mutter something noncommittal. I’d like to get through my first week in this new town—new apartment, new school, new support group—without adding anything else to my already-uprooted life. Please and thank you.

The show has me mesmerized from the moment the curtain rises. I’m familiar with the characters—Cinderella, Jack and his beanstalk, a wicked witch, a baker and his wife, Little Red Riding Hood, two handsome princes and a big bad wolf—but the way their stories are interwoven is pure magic. Within moments I find myself laughing … but later I find tears slowly trickling down my cheeks. The whole thing is heartfelt and wonderfully acted. I've been to theatre in Boston and New York, so I know that these are topnotch performances. Theatre at its finest.

For one brief moment—totally immersed in the story—I reach out my right hand to clasp Marc's, like I often did when sharing a theatre experience like this. But of course, he isn't there. Luckily, no one is sitting beside me and I find myself clutching the wooden arm of my seat instead.

The lights go on after the Narrator calls out the last words of the first act, "to be continued!" Still moved by the power of the way the characters' stories came together, giving each one a happy-ever-after ending, I linger in my seat while others converse during the ten-minute break between acts.

I used to believe in happy-ever-afters, but I've been through so much these last two years that I know they aren't real. By the end of the first act, everyone on stage had taken the difficult journey "into the woods" and returned with exactly what they wished for. Cinderella had her prince. Jack was rich and had his best friend, the cow. The Baker and his wife had their baby. Little Red Riding Hood was safe from the wolf.

But then, the curtain rises on Act Two. Time has gone by and our fairy tale friends' "happy-ever-afters" are not as wonderful as they thought. Cinderella's prince has a wandering eye. The giant at the top of Jack's beanstalk is downright angry. The Baker loses his wife. Little Red can't find her granny.

Through the laughter and the tears, I've felt something subtle inside of me shift. Nothing in life is ever exactly the way we imagine it to be. How could it be? We are always changing, and life always seems to throw obstacles in our path, no matter where we are on our journey, and sometimes those obstacles show up in the way of loss. What was that line in one of the songs? *Sometimes people leave us halfway through the woods.* Unfortunately, I know that to be true. But isn't it also true that our journeys can be interrupted by what we *find* in addition to what we lose?

As I'm pondering the meaning of love and loss after the final curtain falls, Bea appears at the end of my row, literally bouncing back and forth from one foot to the other. "Elena, love! Come with me! There's someone I want you to meet. Hurry now! He's waiting backstage."

I follow her nervously across the front of the theatre and up the steps at stage right, wondering who "he" is and why we're going backstage to meet him. If Bea is playing matchmaker with me … I shudder at the thought and pull my sweater tightly around me. Yes, I know I told the TNA group the other day that I might want to meet someone, but I was thinking it would be on my own terms, not someone else's. And certainly not this soon.

She leads me backstage to a large room with several comfy mismatched sofas and a kitchen area off to the side. There's a young man grabbing a soda from a battered old fridge and Bea calls to him, "Ryan, get your bum over here, darlin'!"

He ambles over to us and throws an arm around Bea like he's known her for years. "Hey Bea! How's it goin'?"

She giggles like a schoolgirl and ruffles his curly blond hair playfully before praising his performance.

"You say that to everyone," he jokes before turning his attention to me. "Now, who is this beautiful woman you wanted me to meet?" I know it's cliché but I pause to catch my breath. I'm face to face right now with the actor who played Jack with such tenderness and unabashed vulnerability.

"This is Elena Jeffries, our new English teacher at the high school and maybe our newest usher." She winks at me and taps my shoulder. "Elena, meet Ryan Summers from New York. He's played Jack before in other prod—." Suddenly, Bea turns her head, noticing that someone across the room is calling her name. "Oh drat, I almost forgot! I've got to take care of something!" She rushes off without another word.

Ryan grins as we watch her leave, sets the soda can down on a nearby table, then takes my right hand in both of his. I'm immediately struck by the rush of energy that travels from his hands to my heart. Along with this energy is a shock of recognition. Somewhere, at some point in my life, I knew someone with this bountiful energy. But who? He is exactly my height but appears about five years younger. Short, curly hair languishes on the border between ash blond and sandy brown, although onstage his hair was red, so he must have been wearing a wig. His wide green eyes are the exact color of the sea glass that Anna held in her hands the other day, and as his eyes meet mine, I can't help smiling. He is slender and good-looking in the way that quirky, creative men usually are—a dead ringer for a young Neil Patrick Harris with slightly longer hair.

"Elena, I am happy to meet you! Thanks for coming out tonight to dress rehearsal. What do you think? Are we ready for opening night tomorrow?"

I am startled by the intensity of his words, and by the effect that being in his presence is having on me, although I can't explain what that effect is exactly. His energy is vibrant and I am caught up in his enthusiasm. The slight melancholy I was feeling as the curtain closed has vanished and in its place is a tiny shimmer of what might be joy. Am I surprised? Indeed, I am. I stumble around for something to say and finally come up with, "You're more than ready! That was an amazing performance."

I begin to look around for Bea to say thank you so I can head home. The large bold-faced clock on the wall shows ten-thirty. Tomorrow is a school day, but my gaze is drawn back to Ryan. For one thing, he's still holding my hand and looking at me as if searching for something. "Thanks for the kind words. There were some little glitches but I don't think anyone but us noticed." He lets go of my hand, pops the soda can open and offers it to me, then takes a healthy swig when I shake my head no. "Tell me, what was your favorite part?"

I'm taken aback by the question, but he seems genuinely interested. "Oh, that's a hard one. I guess the part that made me laugh the most was when the princes sang about their agony."

Ryan chuckles and nods in agreement. "Everyone likes that part. So clever."

"Yes, it helped to have some lighter moments among all of the … loss."

"I agree! It's what makes this show absolutely genius. Stephen Sondheim … " He shakes his head and sets the soda can back down. "The man is freakin' brilliant."

"Also, the scene near the end, when you and Cinderella and the Baker and Little Red are singing the song about how we're never alone. That was moving." I tap my heart lightly.

He is looking at me thoughtfully, and I have no idea what is on his mind. Can he see the loss—the loss that has defined me for the last two years—written on my face? "It's one of my favorite parts too," he replies. "Bea said you're new to Seahaven?"

I look into his eyes and I'm shocked to find that I feel so comfortable with him. "That's right. I'm from Boston. And … you're from New York?"

"The Big Apple herself. I'm originally from Michigan but I'll never go back."

I don't see Bea anywhere. There are actors and backstage folks coming and going, calling "great show" and "good night" to Ryan and each other. He acknowledges them but keeps his gaze fixed on me.

Maybe it'll be okay to stay and talk with him a little longer. "How are you liking small town Seahaven?" I ask.

He touches my arm lightly. "I love being this close to the ocean, that's for sure. It seems like a great little town. How about you?"

"I haven't been here very long, but … so far, so good."

Ryan bounces on his toes a few times, then glances around. Bea truly has disappeared, along with almost everyone else. "Let's grab a drink or a cup of coffee. I'd like to keep talking with you."

His eagerness is apparent and it feels like he might still be channeling some of the fairy tale Jack's youthful exuberance, but I'm caught unaware by the invitation and land back in real time and space with a mental thud. "Oh, I don't think … " Now I'm swallowing hard and stuttering like an idiot. "I mean, thank you, but I need to get up early tomorrow. It's a school day."

"Okay, I hear you," he replies gallantly, still holding me with his gaze. "Maybe another time?"

"Maybe," I say, slowly moving away from him.

"How about Monday?" he calls after me.

I turn. "I have to teach."

"What about after school? We could grab a bite to eat. Maybe take a walk?"

What is happening right now? There's no way I'm going out with this stage actor from New York. Yes, it's true that there is something undeniably charming and authentic about Ryan, but his focused attention combined with his high energy is making me a little bit dizzy. "Sorry, that's probably not a good idea." It sounds lame, even to me, but there you have it. I thought I might be ready, but it's apparent now that I am *not* ready for this. Whatever *this* actually is.

# *Chapter 4*

*"So? How has* it been in Seahaven?" Camille's comforting face gazes at me through the Zoom screen on my laptop. Camille had urged me to make this move, right along with Carlos. I had agreed, but only if I could stay in touch with her, so we arranged these monthly Zoom appointments instead of in-person weeklies.

I am sitting on the back deck of the apartment building, looking out over a wide expanse of recently-mowed lawn between here and Kit's cottage. It's the first Saturday of September but the usual New England autumn chill hasn't found us yet. I wonder if the winters are harder an hour north of Boston. My thoughts have been wandering, but Camille is still speaking. "You've been there a few weeks, right?"

"Almost," I reply, drinking slowly from my *Teachers Do It With Class* water bottle (a treasured birthday gift from Marc) as I admire her no-nonsense, short gray hair and keen blue eyes. "It's been … okay, I guess."

"Tell me more."

"I like it here. The kids in my classes are attentive, for the most part. The apartment is nice, and I like living closer to Carlos." I screw the cap back onto the bottle.

"Have you made any friends? Joined any groups? Done anything fun?"

Ah, yes. I knew Camille would ask me this. From day one, she was always challenging me to try new things on my own. I clear my throat. "I'm focusing on my classes right now. Trying to get my bearings, you know?" Camille nods. "I went to that grief support group the other day. Remember? I told you about it and you encouraged me to go? I went with Kit Gilmore, who owns the apartment building I'm living in. It's called Together Not Alone. TNA."

"Oh yes, I remember now. Great name for a support group!" Camille perks up, tapping her fingers on the edge of her elegant armchair. "Was it helpful?"

"A bit." I close my eyes.

"Go on."

I meet her gaze through the screen and it feels like she is here with me instead of ninety miles away in her Brighton, Massachusetts office. "It feels strange to talk about … all of this … with a circle of people instead of only you."

"I understand. Did you share about Marc? And everything else?"

"I told them about Marc," I reply, looking away from her curious gaze. "I can't talk about … the rest of it. Not yet, not with strangers. It's one loss too many."

Camille nods and steeples her fingers together in a gesture of infinite patience.

"Another cool thing happened this week," I say in an attempt to change the tender subject of what I'd lost in addition to Marc. I don't want her nagging me about it again.

"Oh?" Camille's eyebrows lift as she leans forward eagerly. "I want to hear."

So I tell her about Bea, Sands of Time Theatre, *Into the Woods*, and meeting Ryan. "He asked me out and I told him no, but I did tell Bea I'd think about becoming an usher." Camille knows that Marc and I loved going to the theatre.

"What a great idea! You'll meet lots of folks that way. Now, why didn't I think of that when you lived in Massachusetts?"

I smile. Camille is an excellent therapist, and I know she's proud of me. It's a wonder that she didn't give me a theatre challenge when I first met her. At the beginning, her challenges were simple. Simple, but not necessarily easy. Go for a walk down the street and back, five minutes tops. Read this book and tell me what you think. Go to a movie alone. A black cat with white whiskers keeps showing up on your doorstep? Invite her in. Give her a name. Let her love you. Better still, let yourself love her.

After a while, Camille's challenges were not so easy. Visit Marc's mother. Donate his clothes to a homeless shelter. Move out of the little house where you and Marc lived for six years (lived, laughed, made love, ate breakfast at noon on Sundays, played badminton in the park down the street, cooked Puerto Rican food together). Move out, start over somewhere new. This is by far the hardest thing I've had to do … besides watching his coffin being lowered in the ground to the sound of his mother's heartbreaking sobs mingled with my own.

I finally figured out that Camille's challenges were meant to be wise ways of moving me into and through my grief. Sometimes I did them right away. Sometimes I resisted and it would take me longer to be ready to do them. I still haven't done the one involving Marc's mother. There is just too much to say and I didn't—still don't—know how to tell her what happened.

"So … you might be a theatre usher and you met an interesting young man." Her familiar voice lifts me out of my memories. "Why didn't you accept his invitation?"

I knew she was going to press me on this so I shake my head adamantly and twist the gold band on my left ring finger. "I'm not ready to date yet. You know that."

"I know no such thing!" Camille frowns and taps her laptop screen. "Maybe you could go back to the theatre or wherever Ryan hangs out and talk with him again."

I sigh and take another gulp of water. I know better than to argue with her. Each of her challenges—the ones I've accepted—have always turned out in my favor. Sooner or later. "All right. I'll talk with him the next time I see him." *If I see him. And I'm certainly not going out of my way to find him.* "Before you get your hopes up, he's five years younger than me."

"Elena, you don't have to marry him! Try reaching out to him and see how it feels. By the way, what show did you see?"

"*Into the Woods*."

"Oh my! That's a good one, fairly laden with stories about love and loss."

"It is."

"Jack's character especially has to deal with the death of his mother."

"And the loss of his best friend, the cow," I add with a smile.

Camille chuckles. "Yes, his mother and his cow. Ryan must be an excellent performer to have landed that role."

"He's talented, that's for sure," I reply. "Carlos's boyfriend, Jasper, works at the theatre too. He told me that they use mostly Equity actors from New York. I haven't been to live theatre since before Marc died and that was to see *Camelot*. I was listening to the soundtrack the other day and I haven't been able to get the song 'Guinevere' out of my head. Do you think there's something symbolic about that?"

"I don't know. Do you want someone to come along and save you?" Camille tilts her head to the left the way she always does when she asks a particularly thoughtful question.

"Save me?"

"Isn't that the song they sing at the end, when Guinevere is tied to the stake and they're about to burn her for committing adultery?"

"Yes, and that part always makes me anxious. Even though Lancelot always shows up at the last minute to save her."

Camille studies me intently. "Are *you*?"

"Am I what?"

"Waiting for someone to save you?"

I stare at her for what feels like an eternity, trying to gather my thoughts. I know that Camille will wait me out on this one, as she's waited so many times before. "I don't know." I've found it best to plead ignorance when I actually *don't* know. I used to try to psychobabble my way out of her questions, but she always saw right through it. "I honestly don't know," I repeat, not able to get the vision of Guinevere out of my head— tied to a stake, surrounded by a jeering, stirred-up, angry crowd, about to die. I felt like that sometimes right after Marc died. There were no jeering crowds, of course, but I felt tied up within myself, no way to escape. No one to save me from the horrifying abyss of loneliness and grief.

Do I feel that way now? Not so much, but how I loved that ending scene of *Camelot*. Lancelot, clad in shining armor, storming past her tormentors, using his sword to cut the ropes that bind her, setting her free. Carrying her off to safety.

"Elena?" Camille's voice carries through my laptop speakers and brings me back to Zoom, back to the picnic table on the back deck of my new home in Seahaven. "You still with me?"

I blink and take a breath. "I'm here. You asked if I was waiting for someone to save me. I don't think so." I glance again at her wise, familiar face. "I know … you're going to tell me that I have to save myself."

"Now, how do you know that?" She clasps her hands behind her head. "Maybe you do need someone to save you."

I resist that thought with every fiber of my being. "No," I say softly. "I don't believe that."

"And yet, is it possible to save yourself? Or do you need others as well?"

I sigh at these new questions. Camille has always been full of questions. Questions that used to exhaust me. Nevertheless, her questions always served to wake me up. Nowadays her questions sometimes amuse me, but they always make me think.

"Save myself? Alone or with others?"

Camille shrugs her do-it-yourself shrug. Her I'll-let-you-figure-that-one-out-for-yourself shrug. "Here's my challenge for next time. Before we Zoom next month, I want you to intentionally seek out Ryan and have another conversation. It sounds like you have some things in common and if nothing else, he could be a friend."

I am frowning and rubbing my forehead. How can I intentionally seek him out without looking like a stalker?

The doubt must show on my face because Camille continues. "I'm suggesting Ryan because you said you felt a connection with him. Now, I'm not saying that you need to fall in love. As we both know, romance is overrated." We both laugh; she has said this to me numerous times. "Let me alter the challenge a bit. I'd like for you to reach out to someone. It doesn't have to be Ryan. Someone at school, the theatre, the support group. Male, female … he, she, they. Are you hearing me?"

"I hear you," I grumble. I haven't had the energy or the inclination to reach out and make a new friend in ages. Most of my friends back in Boston were couples that Marc and I hung out with. After he died, they were there for a while, but I was always the third wheel. Last year, they tried fixing me up with their single male friends, but I wasn't interested and they (or was it I?) slowly drifted away. Most people my age haven't experienced this kind of loss, which feels like a huge barrier to me.

Camille and I set the date for our next appointment and I close my laptop, gazing across the lawn at Kit Gilmore's cottage which is painted the same buttery yellow as this Victorian. I'm staring into space, trying to absorb Camille's latest challenge, when I see Kit strolling around the corner, hands in the pockets of her long, flowered skirt. She seems to be in another world, unaware of her surroundings. As I'm wondering what she's thinking about, she notices me on the patio and stops abruptly. Kit's smile is genuine, although I'm sure my presence startled her. "Hey, Elena! I've been meaning to ask about the rest of your first week at school. May I join you?"

I nod politely, half wishing I was still alone with my thoughts, but as she sits across from me at the picnic table, I notice that part of me is glad for her company. "So?" she says, leaning her elbows on the table as if I'm about to share the best bit of gossip. "How was it?"

"Very good. I'm taking some time to get to know the kids and find my way around."

"That sounds just right. You'll let me know if you need anything?"

"Sure, thanks."

Kit sits on her hands and looks across the lawn. There are several towering pine and elm trees bordering the yard, and her garden shows off an inspiring display of cheerful sunflowers and purple asters. Autumn will be here soon, but right now the grass and garden are still lush and green. "I'm so glad you decided to move here, and to take this apartment." She gestures upward.

"Carlos and Jasper told me it was empty for a long time?"

"Yes, almost two years."

This seems strange to me because the landlords I've known in the Boston area usually have apartments filled the day after a tenant leaves. "Why wait that long to rent it out?"

"Good question! You may have heard that I'm a firm believer in the magic of synchronicity."

I shift in my seat, a little uneasy … but curious. "I know what synchronicity means. Jung wrote about it, if I'm remembering correctly."

"That's right."

"But what does it have to do with leaving a perfectly good apartment empty for two years?"

She is smiling brightly now; her earlier inner focus seems to have shifted. "It's a matter of waiting for the right tenant to come along."

"That makes sense, but how did you know I was the right tenant?"

"Oh, dear girl, I just knew." Kit adjusts the apple-green scarf around her neck. "It's a feeling that I get … inside." She stands and places her hands on her solar plexus. "Right here. An inner knowing, you might call it. The same feeling that I got when I heard that Jasper needed a place several years ago, and when my niece Tess was in a difficult situation in Connecticut. I don't believe that one of my apartments being empty at the exact right time was a coincidence for any of them. Synchronicity was at play."

"And me?"

Kit stands beside me, placing her hand on my shoulder. "As soon as Jasper told me that Carlos's sister was moving to Seahaven, I immediately knew that the empty apartment was for her. For you." She kisses me on the top of my head, and I smile at the tender touch. When was the last time someone kissed me like that? "You might want to come to one of my classes at Coastal Soul sometime."

"Maybe." My reply is quick because I know it's what she wants me to hear. "Kit?" I say as she's stepping down from the patio and onto the freshly-mowed lawn.

"Yes dear?"

"A few minutes ago, when you came around the corner, you seemed lost in thought. Is something on your mind?"

She places her hands on her cheeks, maybe to hide the flush that's creeping up from her slender neck and onto her face. "How kind of you to notice." She looks over her shoulder at her cottage, then sits across from me again, reaches into the pocket of her skirt, pulling out a pack of cigarettes and a lighter. "Sorry, bad habit," she says as she lights a slim cigarette and inhales deeply. I feel grateful when she purposely exhales away from me. "I was thinking about a couple of things. First, how much I'm missing Lillian."

"I remember. You talked about her at TNA this week."

"Yes, I used to call her my almost-mother-in-law. Ollie's mom. She was more like a mother to me than my own. I miss her dreadfully."

"I'm sorry," I murmur. Kit is experiencing a different kind of loss, but one that's no less difficult to carry.

"Thank you, Elena. I'll be okay. It's taking a while to get used to her … absence."

We sit in silence for a few minutes. Finally, Kit stubs out her cigarette on the concrete patio floor. She places the butt in a small ceramic bowl in the center of the table and clears her throat. "Also, since you asked, I've been preoccupied lately with some thoughts about the man I've been seeing."

This gets my attention. Kit has a boyfriend? "I'm listening."

She seems flustered, which —even though I haven't known her very long—seems out of character. "His name is Marshall Sorenson. He's a talent agent in New York City. Actually, he was my agent … many moons ago."

"That's right. Carlos told me you were a model?"

She nods.

"And this … Marshall. You've been with him since then?"

"Oh, heavens no!" Kit laughs lightly. I like the way her eyes crinkle up. "His wife died last year, and he drove up here to visit me last month. So … it's all rather new … and strange, I must say."

Something about her hesitation makes me like her even more. "But you really like him?"

"We've always been friends," she replies thoughtfully. "Even when he was married. It took me many years to get over Ollie. I've had male companionship over the years, of course, but my heart does get lonely from time to time. And yes, I really like Marshall. He's about to retire and might be moving up here."

I tuck my laptop under my arm as I stand. "Hmmm … I guess you could say it's quite *synchronistic* that he's started reaching out to you at this time." I hope she understands the teasing tone in my voice.

It appears she does because she breaks into hearty laughter again. "You could say that," she replies, waving me off as we both go our separate ways.

# Chapter 5

*I was hoping* to get up early this morning to watch the sunrise, but it's raining and quite chilly, so I slept in. Now I'm heading to Simply Coffee for a hit of caffeine and maybe something sweet. I hear they have excellent baked goods. Carlos told me that the shop is owned by Fred and Samuel—aka Framuel—two older men who are longtime Seahaven residents. It seems that at two o'clock, they flip the Simply Coffee sign over and the shop becomes Simply Sweets, at which point they put away the coffee and baked goods, and start serving nothing but the best homemade ice cream. Evidently, if you want homemade ice cream before two o'clock, you need to head ten miles up the coast to Waker's Beach, and if you want Framuel's special roast coffee or baked goods *after* two, that's just too bad. A bit gimmicky, in my humble opinion, but who am I to judge?

It's a little after ten when I claim a table by the window and set up my laptop along with a big stack of "What I Wish I'd Done on My Summer Vacation" essays. I always look forward to reading these. Some make me laugh out loud and others bring sadness to my heart because I can feel the longing in a student's words, a longing for something better. Before reading, I'm going to catch up on email, but first… coffee!

There are several people scattered around the large, brightly-lit space. Some are sitting together and chatting quietly, sipping coffee from large blue and white striped ceramic mugs. A few others sit alone, tapping at their phones, munching on muffins or scones. As I head to the counter, I stop suddenly when I see Ryan Summers intently talking on his phone a few tables away. He's wearing jeans and what looks like a much-worn, cranberry-red *Godspell* tee. My stomach does an uncharacteristic flip at the sight of his lanky body and light hair. I'm attracted to him, but do I want him to know it? Do I want to let *myself* know it? Maybe I can scoot on by before he sees me.

Suddenly I remember Camille's "challenge." At the same time, Kit's words about synchronicity float into my brain. Interesting.

As I walk closer to his table, I notice a large bowl of what appears to be coconut chocolate chip ice cream in front of him. This surprises me because it's nowhere near two o'clock in the afternoon.

My place in the ordering line lands me right beside his table. When Ryan's eyes meet mine, his face lights up in recognition. He holds up a finger, inviting me to wait. "Hey Wendell, gotta run," he says into his phone. "Call you back in a bit, okay?" He listens, still smiling. "Sure, no problem." At this, he sets the phone face down on the table, and meets my eyes. "So glad to see you again. Elena, right?"

I nod, strangely happy as I regard his open, friendly face.

"Join me?" He indicates the empty seat on the other side of his table. "That was my agent on the phone. He can wait." Ryan swirls his spoon through the half-melted ice cream.

Hesitant, I continue to stand, glancing at the order line which has moved away from me. I really do want that coffee, but I'm starting to think that maybe I want this connection a tiny bit more. He's looking at me so eagerly, it's like he's already forgotten that I turned him down a few days ago. "I'll sit with you if you tell me how it is that you can get ice cream on a Sunday morning in this place that never, *ever* sells it before two o'clock."

Ryan puts his hand over his heart and pretends to pout, then offers me a dramatic stage whisper. "I told Framuel that if I didn't get a dish of this delectable goodness right away, it would affect my *Into the Woods* performance."

"And you couldn't possibly wait four more hours." *Am I actually flirting with him?*

"Absolutely not." He's grinning mischievously now. "Go get a spoon and I'll share."

"No fair! You're using your celebrity status in Seahaven to get Framuel to break the rules!"

He shrugs good-naturedly as he takes a spoonful of the pale ice cream that is studded with almonds and chocolate chips. When the spoon is empty, he playfully waves it at me. "We do what we have to do," he replies playfully, gesturing again to the empty seat across from him. "Seriously, please join me?"

I look across the shop at my lonely table by the window and his head turns in the same direction. "Unless I'm infringing on something else? Papers to grade?"

Bringing my gaze back to him, I sense a natural openness flowing from him, hovering in the air all around us. It feels welcoming and safe here at this table. Our banter somehow feels familiar, and his liveliness is sparking something inside of me, some memory … not of Marc. No. Marc wasn't this charismatic, this compelling; he had his own unique energetic vibe. Being with Ryan reminds me of something or someone else, but I can't quite put my finger on what or who that might be.

"I do need to read some essays," I say, feeling my hesitation slough away along with my Sunday-morning loneliness. "But I have all day for that. Give me a minute to move my things and get my … " I look at him and his ice cream pointedly. "Coffee.

Since I have absolutely no influence whatsoever on Framuel to order anything *else*."

He laughs and the laughter continues after I join him with my coffee, the stack of papers, laptop, and something called a "scuffin." In fact, I can't remember the last time I laughed this much. He entertains me with stories featuring some of his cast members and a few goof-ups during opening night: the cow tipping over ahead of time, the wolf's "head" separating from the rest of the costume, sound effects not happening at the right time. "It went much smoother last night, but the matinee was a little rough." By now he has finished his ice cream and is leaning forward, elbows on the table, gaze fixed on me. It's almost as if there's no one else in the shop, although I can tell by the hum of voices that more people have entered.

"I didn't notice anything wrong at dress rehearsal." My coffee is cool enough now to take more than a sip, so I indulge along with a bite of this scuffin which turns out to be a glorious blueberry-studded concoction that's not quite a scone and not quite a muffin.

"It's such a complex show, you know? I'd be surprised if everything went perfectly right from the start. Had you seen *Into the Woods* before our dress rehearsal? Do you love theatre as much as I do?"

"I do love theatre, but not enough to be *in* a performance, like you. At my old school in Massachusetts, I did some directing. High school plays, you know. That was fun. As for *Into the Woods,* your dress rehearsal was the first time I've seen it, and I think I'd like to see it again."

"Excellent. I can get you comps, just let me know when."

"Wow, thanks."

Ryan plays with the wooden napkin holder on our table. "So, Elena, what's your story?"

"My story?" I set my scuffin down (what's left of it) and brush the crumbs off my hands. I know darn well what he means, but do I want to tell him … everything?

"Yeah. Bea said you're teaching high school English and it's your first year here, so where were you before and why did you move here?" He nods to my left hand. "Also, you seem alone, yet you're wearing a wedding ring."

"Oh. Right." I've been looking around the shop but now I meet his gaze. They say that some people wear their heart on their sleeve; Ryan seems to wear his in his eyes … and I can see that his heart is listening.

I tell him my story. Most of it, anyway. My marriage to Marc, his death, my almost-two years of grieving and putting my life back together, the job opening in Seahaven, Carlos and Camille urging me to start over here. The other thing … I can't get that part of the story out, but it's okay. He's been listening intently; he didn't even look away when several cast members came in laughing and carrying on loudly.

Now he's reaching across the table and taking my hand—the one that's been clutching my coffee mug handle. My cold fingers gladly absorb his warmth. "That's a lot to go through," he says softly. "I'm sorry about Marc."

I stare at my hand in his. If you'd told me yesterday that I'd be holding hands with Ryan this morning, I would have said *no way*. But here I am, and I'm surprised to find that I rather like it. "Thank you." My voice is a bit hoarse. I glance at my phone and realize it's almost eleven o'clock. "I really should get going on these papers." I let go of his hand and tap the top essay on my orderly pile.

"Okay, sure. I see that some friends have arrived." He waves at his cast mates seated a few tables away. "I'll never hear the end of it if I don't join them for a few minutes, so I'll leave you to it.

But I want to ask you … We've got a show this afternoon, but I'm free tonight and all day tomorrow. Can we get together tonight or maybe tomorrow after you get out of school? I'd love to spend more time with you."

Part of me wasn't expecting his invitation, but I'm aware that another part of me would have been deeply disappointed if he had simply stood up and walked away. "Yes, I'd like that. I have plans with my neighbor Kit tonight, but tomorrow after school would be great."

Ryan smiles broadly and cheerfully slaps his hand lightly on the table. "Awesome!" He points at my phone. "Let me give you my number. Call me when you're out of school and we'll make plans."

After exchanging numbers, I watch him hurry over to his friends' table. They make room for him and he is instantly absorbed into their camaraderie. I eavesdrop on their hearty banter for a few minutes before opening my laptop and focusing on my email. I want to let Camille know that it only took me two days to meet her latest challenge.

My Sunday night plans with Kit involve a light supper of Caesar salad and grilled chicken in her cottage. For some reason, she has taken a liking to me and I'm glad because I'm drawn to her easy warmth and kindness. Her home is cozy and quaint; the kitchen is decorated in soft blues and sunny yellows, and she's wearing a cerulean blouse that makes her seem a part of the decor. There's a tall white candle lit in the center of the table which is covered with a white cloth embroidered with sunflowers.

Before sitting down, Kit sets teak bowls of salad at our places and indicates a platter of grilled chicken. "Help yourself. I forgot to ask you yesterday how the dress rehearsal went. I've always loved *Into the Woods.* In my humble opinion, Stephen Sondheim is a genius."

"It was absolutely brilliant, and I agree about Sondheim."

We tuck into our salads. The room is quiet except for our munching and the last remnants of birdsong outside the bay window. "Lots of pain and loss in those characters' stories, eh?" she finally says, setting down her fork and looking at me, eyebrows raised.

"Yes, but lots of laughter too."

"I'm glad you noticed the fun parts."

"Oh my gosh! I love a show that makes me laugh and cry in equal amounts. How many times have you seen it?"

Kit spears a piece of grilled chicken and places it on her greens. "So many, I've lost count! I've seen it on Broadway, London, and locally." She slices the chicken and pops a piece in her mouth. "I also own the DVD of the original Broadway version."

"I'm hoping to see it again. Bea introduced me to Ryan—he plays Jack—and he said he'd get me tickets. Maybe you can go with me."

"I would love that, dear!"

"Do you have a favorite part?"

"Hmmm … " Kit sets down her fork and reaches for her water glass. "So many. I do love it when the princes sing 'Agony'."

"Me too! I laughed so hard at that one."

"And even though it happens at a sad part of the show, I do like it when Cinderella, the Baker, Jack, and Little Red Riding Hood come up with the plan to slay the giant. They all work together, even though the Baker was thinking he would go on his way alone."

I take another piece of chicken and slowly slice it into bite-size pieces. "It's Cinderella's idea, isn't it? To get the birds to help them blind the giant?"

"That's right." Kit smiles. "And I love the part where Little Red sarcastically says, 'You can talk to birds?'"

"I laughed out loud at that one," I reply, biting into some salty romaine. "Thank you for supper. This is delicious."

She shrugs and offers me a wedge of Italian bread. "I'll be the first to admit, I'm not a great cook. If it's simple, I can do it. If it's not, forget it! What about you? Do you like to cook?"

"I used to like to make some of my mom's recipes. She was Puerto Rican, so we grew up with dishes like tostones and picadillo. I haven't cooked much since … you know." Kit nods sympathetically. "I'm like you now. The simpler, the better."

"And how are you settling in? The apartment? Life in Seahaven?"

I set down my fork and study her for a moment. Last month, when Carlos put me in touch with her about the apartment, we were complete strangers … and now she's an important part of my life. I have no idea how that happened exactly. Technically, she's my landlady, but she seems to be taking me under her wing. I don't think she has children of her own—although she is close with her niece Tess—and I don't have a mother anymore. Perhaps we are filling an important need for one another. "I'm feeling more settled by the day," I reply, wiping my mouth with a daffodil-yellow cloth napkin.

"Do I detect a note of happiness in your voice?" Kit sips from her tall glass of ice water. Her tone is teasing and light.

Not sure how to respond, I gulp my own drink, then carefully cut another strip of chicken.

"I'll cut to the chase, dear. I'm good friends with Framuel and they told me that you seemed to be having a good time this morning with a certain cast member from *Into the Woods*."

My cheeks immediately heat up but she is smiling at me encouragingly, so I tell her more about Ryan, the ice cream, the way he listened to part of my story, and our plan for tomorrow afternoon. "I'm a little nervous," I admit. "It's been a long time since I've been in the world of dating."

"I haven't met Ryan yet, but if he's playing the character of Jack, he's got to be mighty talented. And hey, I can relate to your nerves." Her gaze drifts across the kitchen to the window that overlooks the lawn between here and the apartments. The sky has darkened already even though it's only a little after six o'clock. Summer is definitely on its way out. "It's a strange feeling, dating again after your beloved is gone. I guess you know what I mean."

I nod. "It's been more than eight years since I've dated. How long ago did… sorry, I can't remember your fiancé's name."

Kit smiles gently and closes her eyes. I imagine memories running through her mind like autumn leaves down a mountain stream. "Ollie. It was short for Oliver. We met freshman year in Orono at University of Maine. 1977. He was from Seahaven."

"And you?"

"I grew up in Brunswick, half an hour north of here."

"Is your family still there?"

She shakes her head, but I don't detect regret or sadness. "My mother and father died within a few years of each other about a decade ago. My brother Frank, Tess's father, is also gone."

"I'm sorry."

Kit opens her eyes and meets my gaze. "Don't be, dear. My mother was … how shall I put it? Not ideal. Although my dad and I stayed close until his passing."

"And Ollie?" I hesitate, unsure if it's okay to continue questioning her like this, but I'm intrigued by her story.

"It was Christmas Eve forty-four years ago that he left us." She shakes her head. "Seems like yesterday. Seems like a lifetime."

"Wow! That's a long time to be without—"

"Oh no, no!" She laughs outright and I'm glad to see her mood has lifted. "There have been other men since Ollie. A few quite serious, but none as perfectly matched, of course. Ollie was my soul mate."

"And this new guy?" I prompt. "Marshall, your former agent?"

"I was nervous when he invited himself up here this summer to the theatre's Gala Anniversary event, but now I look forward to more of his visits. And I bet you'll be fine after your first date with Ryan too."

"I sure hope so." I take the last bite of a garlicky crouton and set down my fork. "I'm attracted to him, but I'm not sure it's physical."

"Oh?"

"It's hard to explain. There's something about him. He's unlike anyone I've ever met. He reminds me of someone, or something, but I can't seem to put my finger on it."

Kit picks up her silverware and stands. "I'm sure it will come to you. Try to stay present and enjoy your time with him."

"We're getting together after school tomorrow but I'm not sure what we'll be doing. I don't know what he's thinking, so—"

"There's no way to get into someone else's head, so don't go trying. Just keep in touch with what *you're* thinking and feeling about him."

"Good advice," I say, settling back in my chair as I wonder if I can really do that.

Kit nods and dreamily glances out the window. I don't know if she's thinking back on Ollie or on what she said about her parents, but I'm content to sit in the silence with her.

# Chapter 6

## KIT GILMORE

### OCTOBER 1977

*"Katharine Marie Gilmore!* Quit gazing off into space and eat your supper."

"Mom, I told you, everyone calls me Kit now." She blinked several times. Yes, she'd been guilty of daydreaming about Ollie instead of focusing on the fresh fisherman's pie in front of her. "Mmm, this smells good," she said, hoping to diminish the rising judgement in her mother's voice.

Jane Gilmore shook her head abruptly and laid her calloused hands flat on the table. "*Everyone else* can call you Kit if they want, but it's way too cutesy for me. We named you after the great actress, Katharine Hepburn, and that is the name you will keep. Right, Carson?" She raised her eyebrows and leveled a hard gaze at her husband.

"Sure, sure. Ayuh." Carson's noticeable Maine accent was never so present as when his wife was trying to start an argument. He bit into a hot flaky biscuit and winked at his daughter. "Katharine. Kit. Kathy. Kitty. I don't cayuh what we call you, s'long as you stay as lovely as you already ah, inside and out."

Kit grinned and enjoyed a bite of the savory pie. "Thanks Dad."

"Who started this whole *Kit* thing anyway?" Jane demanded, swirling the ice in her water glass but not drinking it.

"Oh, that would be her new boyfriend, *Ollie*," teased Kit's brother, Frank. Kit kicked him under the table and he grinned. Frank was three years older than Kit and starting his senior year at University of Maine Orono (UMO) while Kit was a freshman. It was Friday night of Columbus Day weekend and they were home for the first time since classes began in September.

"Ollie?" snapped Jane. "You're dating someone named *Ollie*? What kind of a name is that for a young man?"

Kit set down her fork. She had anticipated nothing less from her stiff, what-will-the-neighbors-think mother. "His full name is Oliver Sean Mattheson and he's from Seahaven." She smiled dreamily again, remembering Ollie's smile, his tender kisses, their frequent, intense conversations about long-term teaching goals and children. Children they would one day teach, and maybe even their own children. Kit knew it was happening fast, but she couldn't help it. Just last night they had said *I love you* to each other while walking back to her dorm after studying at the library.

Her father interrupted her reverie. "Frank, have you met Kit's new beau yet?" Carson chewed heartily as his gaze landed on his son.

"Yeah, Ollie's all right I guess." He grinned mischievously at his sister.

"All right? He's more than all right! He was valedictorian at Seahaven High *and* got a full scholarship to UMO. He's the nicest person I've ever met—smart, thoughtful, and kind. We met in Educational Psychology class our first week and we've been together ever since." She noticed her mother's raised eyebrows and was quick to amend her statement. "Not *together*-together, of course." She knew her mother's views on premarital relations.

"This Ollie of yours. Is he studying to be a teacher too?" Carson prompted as he slathered butter on another biscuit and popped a huge piece in his mouth.

Kit nodded as she speared a scallop with her fork and chewed thoughtfully. The salty freshness of the seafood made her smile. She loved her mother's seafood pie. "Yes. High school English. He loves to read as much as I do, can you believe it?" She giggled.

"That *is* hard to believe," Carson replied with a smile, wiping his mouth with a napkin. "My girl does love her books."

Jane smiled stiffly. "You'd better keep to your studies and put dating on the back burner for now. No need to get serious, Katharine. You're too young for that nonsense. Psychology, eh? Don't start thinking that you know more than we do about children and such. Book learning and classes are one thing. Experience is quite another. Carson, Frank? Do you want more pie? I've got another warming in the oven."

"I'll have some!" Frank jumped up and headed for the kitchen.

"Count me in," Carson called after him.

"Mom, don't worry. Ollie and I are taking it really slow. And I promise to rely on your experience with the little ones as soon as I get a kindergarten classroom of my own."

"I haven't been a teacher, but I do know something about little ones because I raised you and Frank," Jane added indignantly.

"I know." Kit sighed, scooping up one last shrimp and a bit of sauce. She raised the fork to her mouth, but it hovered there as she once again gazed off into space. She wondered what Ollie was doing right now. He lived in Seahaven, a beautiful small town farther south on the Maine coast. Her family had gone there once years ago but she didn't remember much about it. She only knew that Ollie loved it there and wanted to teach at Seahaven High after graduation. Ollie. Handsome, kind, tender-hearted Ollie. Super-tall Ollie with the curly brown hair and hazel eyes that reminded her of golden sunlight shining through the boughs of an evergreen tree. Even though Kit had just met him five weeks ago, she felt like she'd known him forever and the best thing was … the feeling was mutual. They were true kindred spirits, exactly like Anne Shirley always talked about in *Anne of Green Gables.*

## CHRISTMAS EVE 1979

"Katharine, wake up!" Jane Gilmore flipped the switch on the overhead light in Kit's bedroom and stood at the door, gripping the beige house phone in one hand. "Katharine! You have a phone call. It's … " She swallowed hard, a sharp anxiety seeping through her words. "It's important."

Kit groaned and shielded her eyes from the glare, glancing at the green neon digits of the clock beside her bed. "Mom," she groaned. "It's four-thirty. I need to sleep." She pulled the pillow over her head as she turned on her side, a lovely length of sandy brown hair spilling across the flowered comforter.

Jane sighed loudly and moved closer to the bed, dragging the extension cord behind her. "I'm not kidding, Katharine." The urgent sharpness in her voice landed somewhere between Kit's brain and her stomach. "Something has happened to Oliver. His mother is on the phone for you."

The words floated around Kit's head like so much mumbo jumbo. *What is Mom talking about? Nothing can happen to Ollie. He's only twenty years old.* Certainly, she must be dreaming. Then, sensing a weighted solemnity behind her mother's words that she'd never heard before, Kit slowly sat up. She stared at her mother, whose mousy hair was tightly wound with curlers and whose face was paler than usual. "Mom? Your hands are shaking."

Jane cleared her throat and tightened her grip on the phone's receiver. "It's Oliver's mother. I've forgotten her name. She needs to speak to you."

Kit felt dizzy with anxiety, but she swung her legs over the edge of the bed and stuffed her feet into a pair of fluffy purple slippers. The old house was chilly on this dark December morning, so she pulled the comforter off the bed and wrapped it around her body, then reached for the phone. Jane handed it to her before moving backwards to stand awkwardly in the doorway.

"Hello?" Kit spoke anxiously into the phone, her right hand tightly gripping the receiver while her other hand fidgeted with the edge of the comforter. She noticed, as if from a distance, the small diamond on her left ring finger and almost smiled. Almost.

"Kit, it's Lillian Mattheson. Ollie's mom."

"Yes, of course. Hi." For some inane reason, she almost blurted out "Merry Christmas," but something deeper, something unknown, stopped her from speaking. There was an awkward silence on the other end of the phone and Kit took a moment to picture Lillian as she had last seen her at Thanksgiving—short and plump, fussing over the guests and food, asking Kit about her classes, talking with Ollie and Kit about their future plans. Lillian was motherly and nurturing, in a way that Jane had never been, which is one of many reasons why Kit loved spending time with Lillian.

"I'm sorry to have to tell you this, Kit, but Ollie … Ollie is … well, he's gone."

Kit stood and began pacing the room, which was difficult because the springy plastic phone cord only stretched so far. She rubbed her eyes with one hand, trying to wipe away this pending nightmare, yet also trying to fathom what Lillian could possibly be saying. "What do you mean? Gone where?" They were planning on going skiing together, but not until after New Year's. Surely, he wouldn't go skiing without her, without his mother and sister.

"I mean, he's … I don't know how else to say this, dear." She stifled a sob. "He's dead."

Kit gasped and almost dropped the phone, but Jane rushed forward to steady it, then handed it back to her. "I don't understand. How? I mean, how could … " She sank to the floor, her nightgown and bulky comforter making a tangled mess around her shaking body.

"He died in his sleep so it was quick and peaceful. He went to bed early, around nine. He looked exhausted, but I thought it was just the stress of exams and end-of-term papers."

"Yes, it was a stressful semester for him," Kit murmured.

"Olivia went into his room after midnight to borrow something or other … I can't remember what … and she noticed that he wasn't breathing." Lillian suddenly stopped talking and Kit could hear her coughing over what sounded like a sob.

She waited not-so-patiently, anxiety growing with every minute, fizzing through every fiber of her body like cold water tossed into a hot frying pan. How could Ollie—her beloved Ollie—be gone? Just like that? "That's not possible," Kit whispered, struggling with every word.

"I'm sorry, dear. It's … I can't believe it myself, so I can't imagine how you must be feeling. Olivia tried CPR but he was … gone. The EMTs came, but it was too late. The medical examiner is with him … with his body now. She thinks it was a rare heart defect. We had no idea."

"No, no, no!" Kit sprang to her feet, discarding the comforter. She was sweating as if it was high noon in August. "You're playing a trick on me, right? Is this some huge joke that Ollie thought up? If it is, please tell him it's not funny!" As her voice intensified to a breathless shout, she noticed a sleepy Frank in the doorway, whispering to their mother. Carson was next to appear at the door.

"Kit! Darling Kit! It's not a joke. We would *never* make something like this up. Listen to me. Is your mother still there with you? You shouldn't be alone."

A huge chill spread through Kit's body as she doubled over, still clutching the phone to her ear. "What?"

"Is your mom there with you? Your dad?"

Kit struggled to grasp the words. Her entire world was cracking wide open and the pain was unbearable. "Mom? Dad?" She looked around the room in a daze, eyes settling on her parents and brother in the doorway. "Yes, they're here."

"Are they all awake? Do they know what happened?"

Kit nodded and dropped the phone to the floor where it landed with a definitive *thud* on the green braided rug. Carson quickly went to his daughter, murmured something into the phone, then hung it up gently and set it aside. He sat on the floor beside his daughter and wrapped his arms around her trembling body. "It's going to be all right, Kit, it's going to be all right."

She heard the words as if whispered from the other end of a gaping canyon, but she couldn't fathom their meaning. Nothing was going to be all right. Ever again.

# Chapter 7

## ELENA

*Kit's suggestion to s*tay out of Ryan's head when I'm with him is easier than I expected because he's always on the move. There's so much more to be aware of than wondering what he's thinking and feeling. It is also becoming apparent that if I want to know what he's thinking and feeling, all I need to do is ask. He is virtually an open book.

On Monday after school, we head over to Wonder Mountain in Moody. I haven't played miniature golf since I was a child, and it's way more fun than I remembered, mainly because Ryan isn't one bit competitive (like Carlos always was). Also, he bursts into song on every other hole. This is the most fun I've let myself have since Marc died, and I'm no longer hesitating to enjoy myself.

We share an Everything Pizza at Blissed Out Pies in Waker's Beach after playing the arcades at Wonder Mountain. When he drops me off on Bright Blessing Way, he kisses me lightly on the lips. "Tomorrow?" he says eagerly as I move to get out of the car, still trying to process the kiss. Ryan's lips don't feel familiar at all, yet they feel good. I'd forgotten what this kind of kiss was like.

"Don't you have a show tomorrow night?"

He smacks his forehead playfully with the palm of his hand. "Of course, that darned show … as if I could forget! I need to be at the theatre at seven, but let's do something after school again. Maybe? Please?" He clasps his hands at his chest in a playfully dramatic gesture. "Do I need to beg?"

I laugh out loud and notice that I'm relishing the sound of my own laughter, which is becoming more and more familiar to me as my days in Seahaven accumulate. "Okay, okay! No need to beg. Meet me here at four and we'll decide what to do."

He agrees and drives off in his rental car. I stand on the sidewalk, watching him wave as he turns the corner.

All day Tuesday at school I find myself thinking about him. Ryan Summers. Curly blondish hair, agile body, lively spirit, green eyes that seem filtered with sunlight. I had planned to focus solely on teaching and my students this year, but a fun-loving, vibrant young man has come between me and my best intentions. Am I complaining? Not at all. I just wish I could remember who he reminds me of.

After school we drive to South Berwick and hike up to Orris Falls. The air has gotten a bit chillier; I can tell autumn isn't far off. He tells me stories about his teenage sister who's been bitten by the theatre bug too, and his pre-med brother in Michigan. He happily talks about other shows he's been in, as well as a few on Broadway that he's auditioned for recently.

In the back of my mind, I know that Ryan isn't going to stay in Seahaven. I have a feeling he is destined for bigger stages than ours. But I listen intently, absorbing the excitement in his voice, and I tell him some of my own stories. How I met Marc. How it rained on our wedding day and the rainbow that appeared as we were leaving the church. Some of the stories that students turned in about their fantasy summer vacations. A few plays I'd directed while teaching in Dorchester. I share a little more about how Marc died, but I don't tell him everything. I don't want to break the cheerful, intimate mood we've created here in this beautiful setting.

Later, I'm finally done with lesson plans and am thinking about bed; Jezebel is cozied up beside me on the sofa. Ryan calls, practically breathless. He's amped up from the performance and wants to come over. My mind is tired but my body surges with a strange yet familiar longing. I brush out my hair, put on a nicer top (this stained Red Sox sweatshirt won't do) and start up the coffee maker.

In the morning, as I get ready to leave for school, Ryan is still in bed.

"Hey, beautiful," he calls as I pull on a denim skirt and long-sleeved red top, pulling my hair away from my face and into a long braid. He appears wide-awake and in full-speed-ahead mode already even though he just opened his eyes seconds ago. I used to be that way too, but since Marc died, it takes me longer to get started when each day begins. Until today. I've already been up for a few hours. In fact, it was still dark when my eyes popped open, so I tugged on my winter coat against the September early morning chill and jogged down to the beach at the end of Bright Blessing Way. There, I watched a breathtaking sunrise whose beauty caught me by surprise. As I walked along the shore, the sky turned several shades of gold and lavender. Like the prettiest watercolor painting, the slowly-emerging sunlight was blurrily reflected in the ripples and rivulets of the low-tide wet sand.

"Good morning." I smile shyly at him from across the room. Jezebel has somehow slipped into the bedroom and is already snuggled against Ryan's legs. Out of the corner of my eye, I notice the boxes of Marc's things sitting by the closet. Perhaps it's time to go through the leftovers of what was his heartbreakingly short life. "I've got to run," I say, sitting on the edge of the bed and kissing him on the forehead. "Seahaven High beckons. Stay as long as you like."

Yawning, he quickly sits up and runs one slender hand through his unruly hair, some of which is sticking straight up. "Thanks!" He pulls me to him in a ferocious hug and the scent of pure male laced with traces of theatrical make-up and cold cream makes me smile again. "For the coffee last night, *and* for everything else. I've never met anyone like you before." He nuzzles my neck and I feel my body stirring … again. Yes, last night was unexpected, in more ways than one. I've definitely never met anyone like him either, yet his presence still feels familiar to me.

As I'm heading to our small parking lot, my brother exits the front door of the apartment building and waves.

"Hey, Carlos! Spending the night with Jasper again?" I tease.

He grins, thoroughly pleased that things with his new boyfriend are going so well. I am equally delighted. Carlos has had a few loves in his life, but they are small compared to what he has with Jasper. Of that we are both sure.

"Yeah, yeah, leave it alone, Sis," he mumbles, heading for his own car. He's wearing the mandatory royal blue Vet Tech scrubs from Bright Side Animal Clinic, a leather jacket thrown over his shoulder. Our hair color is identical—ink black—but his is as curly and short as mine is straight and long but we share the same dark brown eyes. He pauses as soon as he notices the rental car parked next to mine. "What about you, Elena?" Curiosity and concern shadow his expression.

I know I'm blushing, but I don't care. "What about me?"

Carlos gestures to the rental car again.

"Ryan came over last night, that's all."

"That's all? Didn't you just meet him last week?" He settles into his car but leaves the door open. After looking in the rear-view mirror to smooth his hair, he glances my way. "I'm not judging, I promise. But it … seems like a big step. Are you okay?"

It's none of Carlos's business, but I understand why my big brother is apprehensive. Even though this is all so new with Ryan, I feel like I've known him a very long time. "I'm finer than fine." My answer begins as an attempt to reassure him, but I realize with a start that it's absolutely true.

My "finer than fine" attitude disappears when I get to school and find myself summoned to Principal Patterson's office at the end of the day. I'm sitting in the small waiting area outside her office, nervously twisting the wedding ring on my left hand when Jonathan MacKenna joins me.

"You too?" he asks as he tries to settle into the stiff plastic chair beside me.

"Me too. Do you know what this is about? I don't think I've done anything wrong yet."

"Not yet," he teases, nudging my arm with his elbow. I haven't seen him since last week in the parking lot when he invited me for ice cream although I've heard some of my students referring to him almost reverently as "Mister Mac." I'd forgotten how clean-cut and attractive he is with his high forehead and short sandy brown hair. He's wearing rectangular tortoiseshell glasses that bring out the green in his hazel eyes. "I may be wrong, but last year around this time, Mrs. Patterson was gathering volunteers for the senior class play."

"Volunteers?"

He laughs and I like the sound of it, deep-throated and unwary. "Yes, we do it for the love of the kids or not at all."

"Did you direct the play last year?"

"Heck, no! Directing's not my thing, but I do know my way around set building and managing props. Last year we did *The Crucible* and the year before that, *Arsenic and Old Lace*. It's fun. I love theatre but prefer to stay *off* the stage!"

"Me too!" I'm pleased at how comfortable I feel with him now, compared to the first day of school which was more than a week ago.

"How about you? My Spidey-sense tells me that at your old school, you directed at least one play, or dare I say … musical?"

"No musicals for me, thank you very much, but I did direct a few at Dorchester High before … I mean, before Marc's accident."

Jonathan doesn't seem unnerved this time by my mention of Marc's death. "What was your favorite show to—"

We are interrupted when Principal Ruby Lee Patterson beckons us into her office. She is as tall as Jonathan—in her mid-fifties I'd guess—with plain brown hair cut in a simple pageboy, no sign of gray. She takes off a pair of thick-rimmed black reading glasses, sets them down on a neat stack of folders, and fixes her dark brown eyes on us. "Elena. Jonathan. Thank you for coming in." Her voice is measured and steady as we sit in cushioned chairs that seem like nirvana compared to what we were sitting on in the waiting area. It's hard to imagine how difficult a principal's job must be, how calm and collected Mrs. Patterson needs to be at all times. Thankfully, school administration is a goal I have never aspired to.

"Our senior class play this year will be *Our Town,* and I'm hoping that you'll consider directing, Elena. I know you've had experience in this area at your old school."

"It's been a few years, so I'm a little rusty." I glance at Jonathan who nods slightly with an encouraging smile. "But sure, I'll give it a go."

"And Jonathan, I hope you'll consider heading up the set-building and props teams again. You did a wonderful job the last few years."

"Happy to, Mrs. Patterson." His response is easy-going and affirming.

She puts her glasses back on, opens a file folder and shuffles through a few papers. "Linnea Blackstone couldn't make this meeting because she's supervising after school cheerleading, but she told me she's all set to help with costumes again." She looks pointedly at Jonathan. "Are you going to be okay with that?"

He shifts uncomfortably in his seat, as if trying to get away from something lodged under the cushion. His eyes are darting uneasily around the office and although he's trying to keep his cool, I can tell there's something going on. Who on earth is Linnea Blackstone and why is he acting this way?

"Jonathan? If you're not comfortable with it, I'm sure we can—"

"I'll handle the costumes," I interrupt. "No problem." Have I ever done costumes for a high school play before? No, I have not. But how hard could it be?

"Are you sure?" She looks a bit bewildered by my sudden offer, but Jonathan turns to makes a slight gesture of gratitude to me with his hands.

"I'm sure." Actually, I'm not sure at all, but I'm willing to try because Jonathan is evidently not okay with working with this Linnea person, whoever she may be.

We set up a schedule for auditions and rehearsals. "Performances will be the second weekend of November," Mrs. Patterson states, closing the folder and standing up as she glances at her watch. "Saturday the eleventh and Sunday the twelfth."

I catch my breath. November eleventh will be the second anniversary of Marc's death.

"That will give everyone time to recover from the Great Big Seahaven Halloween Scavenger Hunt," Mrs. Patterson continues.

Jonathan and I stand and make our way to the door. "I've not heard about that yet," I say to her over my shoulder.

"Oh, you will!" she replies, her eyes crinkling into a wide smile.

In the office as I'm checking my mailbox and shrugging into a jacket, Jonathan taps me on the shoulder. "Hey, thanks for saving my butt in there."

"Sure," I murmur, hoping that I can somehow manage to direct the play, find all the costumes, and work the fittings in too. Not to mention being able to be totally present at our opening night while still holding Marc's memory close.

"I'll help you with the costumes," he says, picking up his briefcase from the office counter. "With the guys' costumes, anyway."

"That'd be great." I'm ready to leave but have the feeling that he wants to tell me something. "Are you okay?" I finally ask.

He sighs and looks briefly over at one of the school secretaries whose head is bent over her keyboard. "I'm okay, but you should probably know that once upon a time, Linnea and I were engaged. The wedding was set for May 18 this year, but … " He smiles awkwardly. "She left me at the altar."

"That's awful! I'm so sorry."

He waves his hand dismissively. "Don't be. It was for the best. Everyone told me she wasn't right for me, but I have a stubborn streak and chose not to listen."

"And now?"

"Now I see how right they were."

"I don't think I've met her. She's a teacher here?"

"Yep. Computer science. Coaches the cheerleading squad after school. She's great with the kids; they all love her."

"But … ?"

"But she's a bit too loud and opinionated for me." He clears his throat and smiles at me again, all awkwardness gone. "So that's the sad story I mentioned in the parking lot last week. Not as sad as yours but—"

"Grief is not a contest," I reply softly. "Sad stories are sad stories."

"Thank you for that. And for listening." He scratches his five o'clock shadow that looks like it's been there since noon. "Also, for agreeing to do the costumes this time around. Hey, I'd like to get to know you better. How about dinner and a movie this weekend? Friday night? Saturday? Or lunch sometime?"

I hear a slight trace of hope in his voice, but any hope that might be swirling around inside of me right now is drowned out by the thought of the last few days and one night with Ryan. I slip my tote bag over my shoulder and look him in the eye. "I'm kind of seeing someone right now, but thanks for asking."

"How do you *kind of* see someone?" he asks, opening the office door for me as we head into the now-empty hallway that smells vaguely of chalk dust, lemon wax, and teenage girls' perfume.

*Good question. How do I answer that?*

"It's complicated," I finally manage. "He's an actor in *Into the Woods* over at Sands of Time. Ryan Summers."

Jonathan contemplates this as we walk down the stairs. The breeze is cool, but the September sun warms our backs. "All right. Two strikes down, one to go," he says with a brief smile and a wave as we each get into our cars which—once again—are parked side by side.

The word *synchronicity* ambles through my brain, then quickly disappears.

I get an understanding of exactly how complicated my relationship with Ryan may be when I have dinner with Carlos and Jasper later that week. We're at an elegant yet welcoming restaurant called Chloe's by the Sea. It's right on the water and we're seated near a window. The sky is darkening into a brilliant sunset.

"Here's to my little sister!" Carlos raises his wine glass in a toast and we join him.

"Cheers!" Jasper sips slowly and savors the Zinfandel. "I'm glad you're here in Seahaven, Elena."

"I'm glad to be here." A few weeks ago, that might have been a rote response, but I realize now that it's true. "What's good here?" I ask, perusing the large single-page menu that is creatively decorated with colorful, bold-stroked art that I see replicated on the table coverings. "And what is this special at the bottom? Chloe's Secret?"

"Everything is good here," Jasper replies. "Especially the seafood, if you're a fan."

I nod.

"As for Chloe's Secret," Carlos says, laying down his menu decisively and picking up his wine glass again. "She only offers it once a week and we never know which day it will be on the menu. If you can guess the secret ingredient, your meal is free *and* you get a free dessert!"

"It's a little gimmicky, but we all love it," Jasper adds.

"If I order it, what will it be exactly?"

"Ah, that's the fun part." Carlos takes a big gulp of wine. "It's always a surprise. Always good, but still … a surprise all the same."

This is a little disconcerting to me. I'm not sure I want to order something sight unseen. It would be like dating someone on one of those apps that my friends back in Massachusetts were hoping I'd try last year. Although, even on one of those apps, at least I could see a picture first. "Have either of you ever ordered Chloe's Secret?"

"I did, a few times," replies Jasper.

"What was it?"

"One time it was this extraordinary seafood stew. A bit like a chowder, but not quite. Another time it was a pesto chicken dish, hard to describe. All delicious."

"Did you guess the secret ingredient?"

Jasper laughs. "No way. My taste buds aren't that good."

When the server comes to our table, none of us order the special dish. *Maybe another time,* I think.

While we're waiting, Carlos points his fork and knife in my direction. "So, Elena … how's it going with Ryan?"

I start to answer but Jasper interrupts. "Ryan?"

"I told you last night. She's seeing Ryan Summers."

Jasper's left hand goes to his throat as if to stop himself from saying something he'll regret. "Ryan Summers, from *Into the Woods*?" he finally manages, moving his hand onto the table and picking up his napkin.

Carlos looks exasperated. "Yes. Ryan Summers!"

Confused, I look back and forth between them. What on earth could be the problem? "Bea Lively introduced us at the dress rehearsal. We've been seeing each other, almost two weeks now."

Jasper clears his throat and looks at me. "It's probably none of my business, Elena, but I know Ryan from the theatre and he's … probably not someone you want to get involved with."

He's right. It really is none of his business, but I can see that it's difficult for him to say this to me.

"Come on, now, Jas." Carlos lays a hand on Jasper's arm. "She deserves a little fun."

"A little fun is all she's going to get." He gulps from his water glass and smacks it down on the table as if to punctuate his thought. "Okay, I'll admit that Ryan's a nice guy, but he's an actor, which means he won't be sticking around. A few more weeks and he's out of here."

"I know this already—" I begin, but Carlos speaks to Jasper first as though I'm not even there.

"Hon, do you think you might be projecting a bit of your relationship with Jake onto Elena and Ryan?" I remember Carlos telling me that Jasper had been in a long-term relationship with a Broadway actor, and that as much as Jasper loved him, Jake wasn't ready to settle down.

Jasper shrugs and fusses with the napkin in his lap. "Maybe. But even if I am, it's never a good idea to get involved with an actor who's always traveling from one theatre to another, from one end of the country to the next." He taps his heart and smiles sadly at me. "That's how hearts get broken, and yours has already been broken in a really big way. I don't want you to get hurt, that's all."

Our server comes with salads for the men and New England clam chowder for me. I watch Carlos and Jasper as the server grinds pepper onto their salads, and say no when she offers the pepper for my chowder. Now that I'm in Seahaven, it seems that I have two big brothers watching out for me instead of just one. I decide that this is not a bad thing.

I wait until our server is gone before saying, "Thank you for looking out for me, Jasper, but I'm okay. Ryan is … " What is he, exactly? I pause and sprinkle some oyster crackers into my chowder, savoring the briny steam that rises from the bowl. "He's good for me right now. I'm a big girl. You don't need to worry."

Carlos deftly spoons some blue cheese dressing over his salad. "We won't worry for now, but if you need us to step in, all you have to do is ask."

I have no intention of asking for their help with Ryan. I already know that this isn't a long-term relationship, and frankly, I don't think I want it to be. But he's helping me to feel things that I haven't felt in years. And that is worth any heartache I might feel when he leaves.

# Chapter 8

*At lunchtime on* Friday, Jonathan and I meet to set up auditions for *Our Town*. He's a perfect gentleman, entirely professional, and doesn't ask me out again. I'm a bit relieved. He seems like a good person to have as a friend, and I know he'll be helpful with the play. He's already sketched out ideas for the set and I've shared some thoughts about the staging, but I need to read the script again over the weekend. It's been a long time since I paid attention to the characters of Grover's Corners.

Aunt Kit knows a great theatrical costume shop in Brunswick, so she's going to drive up there with me tomorrow. She also volunteered to help with hair and make-up at dress rehearsal and during the performances. I'm grateful because I wasn't sure where to begin, and I don't know much about make-up—I hardly wear anything but mascara and lip gloss—much less stage make-up. When I told her about Jonathan and Linnea last night, she knew all about the wedding that never happened. I guess in a small town like this, word gets around.

Ryan comes over again after the show tonight and we stay up late talking and drinking coffee. Do I need caffeine at this hour? I do not. However, it's the weekend and I don't have to get up early for school tomorrow. Besides—Ryan is a lot of fun to stay awake with.

I haven't pulled an all-nighter like this since college. The coffee is hyping me up, and Ryan … well, Ryan's energy is always contagious, with or without caffeine. However, I'm happy to report that he does slow down a bit when we're kissing.

Now I'm lying on the comfy sofa, my legs stretched across his lap. Jezebel is purring contentedly, curled up between us, as I luxuriate in the pleasure of Ryan's hands massaging my left foot. "Do you think this was destiny?" I ask lazily.

"You mean us … meeting now … at this particular point in our lives?" His fingers pause.

"Right. What if I'd never moved to Seahaven? Or what if they'd given the part of Jack to someone else?"

"And what if Bea hadn't insisted on dragging you backstage to meet me?" He grins and begins massaging my other foot.

"Ryan, be serious. What if—"

"We can't live our lives around *what ifs*, can we?" He closes his eyes and leans back against the cushions, one hand still resting on my happily-satisfied feet, the other hand on a purring Jezebel.

"No," I reply carefully, drawing out the word as I contemplate his statement. "But I feel like I've known you forever, or in another life maybe. I can't imagine what my life would be like if I hadn't met you when I did."

"I can't imagine that either. But destiny? I don't know." He's staring at the ceiling now and shaking his head. "I've never believed in destiny. I've always done what I felt I needed to do next with my life. And God, or the universal forces … or something … takes care of the rest. I don't think it's all planned out ahead of time."

"Oh."

"Don't you live that way too?" he asks, gently pushing my legs off the sofa and pulling me over so I'm nestled against him. Jezebel meows plaintively at being disturbed, and jumps onto my lap. "Becoming a teacher, marrying Marc, letting Jezebel into your life, moving up here away from the city, accepting Bea's invitation to the dress rehearsal?"

I rest my head on his shoulder. "I became a teacher because I love books and reading and teenagers. I married Marc because I fell in love with him. I let Jezebel into my life because Camille told me to, and I moved up here because Carlos and Camille thought I should. I was perfectly happy to let them make decisions for me after Marc died."

Ryan strokes Jezebel's sleepy head. "What if Camille had told you to quit teaching and go to law school?"

"That's ridiculous."

"Or what if she'd said, 'Throw that black cat out on the street because she'll bring you bad luck'?"

"Camille would never—"

"That's right, she wouldn't. My point is—*you're* the one who chose Camille. She didn't come and pick you out as a client. *You* decided to open the door to Jezebel, even though it was Camille who suggested it." At the sound of her name, Jezebel lifts her sleek black head and blinks at me as if to confirm Ryan's words. "And *you're* the one who chose to move here. *You* made the decisions, you took the action steps, even though others offered their opinions."

I lift my head and tenderly kiss Ryan on the cheek. "I think you may be right."

"I've been told from time to time that I am very wise," he says with a teasing smile as I swat him on the arm.

"What you're saying is … we choose what we think is best for us in the moment and live with the outcomes." I shift away from him and start tugging on my socks and shoes. "Which isn't destiny at all, right? We're creating our own destiny as we go."

"Exactly. I mean, take Marc for instance. You don't believe it was his destiny to die before his life was even half over, do you?"

"Definitely not," I say slowly, standing and stretching as I ponder this thought. A year ago—heck, even a month ago—I would have had to reach for a big box of tissues when reminded of Marc's death so blatantly. But now I simply feel the ache of that space. It's like Anna said at the TNA group: my heart seems to have grown bigger in order to make room for my sorrow, so the sharp edges of grief don't keep pressing up against my memories. "You know, Kit talks a lot about synchronicity. Maybe there's a fine line between that and destiny." I gently set Jezebel back on the sofa, take Ryan's hands and pull him up. Holding his face in my hands, I murmur, "Either way, I'm glad we met when we did."

"Me too." He kisses me and turns toward the bedroom, but I pull him back. "Let's go outside and watch the sunrise."

Ryan looks surprised, then smiles agreeably and grabs his leather jacket as we head for the door.

In the cool morning-star dark of late September, walking side by side with Ryan lights up my spirit with wonder. At first, we stroll quietly, thinking our own thoughts in our own little worlds, my right arm hooked through his left. I feel at peace with myself. Grounded. Trust me, I haven't felt like this in a very long time. Not since Marc. And even though Ryan is not Marc—he's nothing like Marc at all—I'm amazed to discover that I like this feeling.

You might be thinking that a few rounds of good lovemaking will do this to a woman, but it's not that. For one thing, Ryan is only twenty-five and could stand to learn a few more things about what women need. Our intimate times together have been satisfying, but I'll be the first to admit that there is something missing. I can't compare it to what Marc and I had together, of course; our relationship was several years in the making, and I am, after all, still wearing my wedding ring. While I find Ryan attractive, it's more of a kindred attraction; I recognize something in him that's been missing in my life. I know that Ryan won't be in my life forever, and I'm okay with that—even if Jasper and Carlos don't understand. I'm simply enjoying each moment with him as it comes. Feeling joy has been strictly off-limits to me for the last two years, ever since Marc died and my world imploded … twice in one month.

As the horizon starts to lighten, Ryan pulls me in for a long kiss, then takes off running like a little boy on the first day of summer. He twirls and dances in between short Olympic-style sprints. I start to run after him, but decide to stop and catch my breath instead. I squat down on the chilled sand to watch him. He's shouting something now, hands cupped around his mouth. Or maybe he's singing. I can't tell exactly, but it makes me happy. His presence has been, and is, skimming cool ripples across the gritty surface of my loneliness.

I stand and walk toward the foamy fingers of water that are etching themselves into the wet gray sand. A ribbon of gold appears on the horizon, then slowly melts into peach and lavender, dispersing the few clouds that hover overhead. Ryan is heading back toward me now, skipping merrily. From a distance, if I didn't know better, he might be ten or twelve years old.

As the first curve of pumpkin-orange sun makes itself known amongst the golden light, I notice something glinting in the sand.

A piece of indigo sea glass, dark as midnight. I bend down to pick it up just as Ryan reaches me. A slight sheen of sweat on his friendly face reflects the light as he bends over to catch his breath. "What did you find?"

I hand it to him and he turns it over. "Sea glass. Also known as beach glass. From bottles or other glassware that have been broken and tossed into the ocean."

"It's pretty." He straightens, and as he holds it up to the rising sun, the deep blue of the glass suddenly becomes a brighter shade of cobalt, like a Caribbean night sky. "Not just pretty," he corrects himself. "Beautiful."

He links an arm through mine and we begin to walk again, heading north along the shoreline, but I stop and face the water. "Let's stand here for a bit and watch," I whisper.

For several minutes we stand, shoulder to shoulder, facing the water as the sun turns from that fiery deep orange to a blinding gold so bright that we need to turn away.

Heading back to Bright Blessing Way, I find a few more pieces of sea glass—one a salty shade of white and another that is a darker green than Ryan's eyes. He appears curious about why I'm so excited to find them, so I tell him what I recently learned about the connection between sea glass and grief. I wonder if there has been any deep sorrow in his life that has ever quelled the joyful light in his eyes, so I ask him.

He shakes his head and takes my hand as we climb the three steps to my apartment building. Settling side by side on the swing at the far end of the porch, he puts his arm around me and I rest my head on his shoulder. He smells like coffee and salt and sand, like a new morning. Like the missing piece of a very difficult puzzle.

"The only people I know who have died are my grandfather Ricky and my mom's brother Devin, but we weren't close. Oh, and a guy in my dorm died from cancer junior year. We ran track together, but it's not like we were best friends or anything."

"So maybe you don't get the part about being broken into pieces?"

"Nah. My mom tells me I've lived a charmed life." I can feel his mouth forming a smile against my temple.

"You're lucky," I reply. What I don't say is that I know he will, eventually, get to that broken place. We all get there, sooner or later. When I was his age, I was living a charmed life too. I'd thought that the worst had happened when my parents died. I had no inkling that there could be much more sorrow around the corner. Neither does Ryan.

"I like the story of the sea glass," he says thoughtfully. "When I'm onstage as Jack and the part in the story comes where the Baker says that my mother is dead, I have to act sad. My imagination is quite vivid, so it's not that hard. My acting coach tells me I'm incredibly emotive." He shifts on the swing and moves his arm from around my shoulder to take my hand. "But it's not the same, is it?"

My words are soft and tender. "No. It's not the same." Even if he can act sad on stage, so sad that audience members brush away their own tears (like I did), he can't comprehend the depth of sorrow that sudden, sharp grief carries with it.

He squeezes my hand and touches my wedding ring lightly. "Could I have one of these pieces of sea glass? I'll keep it in my pocket as a reminder that even when grief comes to me—and I'm guessing it will—its sharp edges won't completely destroy me."

"Of course. Here, take all three." I reach into my jacket pocket and hand them over.

"No, thanks. One is enough." He plucks the milky white glass from the trio and cups it in his palms. "Thank you."

I'm about to suggest heading back inside for breakfast—or perhaps sleep—when Kit approaches from the sidewalk, lost in thought. She's dressed in purple yoga leggings and a heavy white cardigan that stretches below her knees. "Good morning, love birds!" She greets us with a hearty salute as she climbs the steps and faces us. "I'm on my way back from a spectacular sunrise. What are you doing up so early?"

"We watched the sunrise too," Ryan says, jumping up and rushing over to shake her hand. "I'm Ryan Summers and you must be the famous Aunt Kit."

"Pleased to meet you, Ryan. You were absolutely wonderful in *Into the Woods*! I've seen the show many times in other places, including on Broadway with Joanna Gleason and Bernadette Peters, and I just love what you did with the role of Jack."

Ryan is no stranger to praise, given how talented he is, but I can tell he's pleased. "Thank you so much. It's always nice to hear from a fan."

"She's not just a fan," I say, getting up from the swing and standing next to him. "She practically runs that theatre."

"Hush, child," Kit replies, waving away my words. "I'm merely on the Board of Directors. By the way, Elena, are we still on for the drive up to Brunswick this morning to the BackStage Costume Shop?" She looks at Ryan. "Did she tell you they've asked her to direct *Our Town* at Seahaven High?"

"She sure did, and I'm going to help with the set building!"

I turn to Ryan, eyebrows raised—this is news to me. He's grinning at Kit who is clapping her hands in delight at the thought of a true theatre professional working on the local high school play.

Jonathan MacKenna has already agreed to manage the scenery, but I suppose it's possible that he could use some help. My mother always used to say that many hands make light work.

I stifle a yawn. "Road trip to the costume shop. Of course. What time do you want to leave?"

She glances between me and Ryan. "I was going to say nine o'clock, but it looks like you might need a nap beforehand, so how about eleven? We'll make an afternoon of it. I can show you where I grew up!"

# Chapter 9

*In the four* hours between saying good-bye to Ryan and leaving for Brunswick with Kit, I take a quick nap, then read through the *Our Town* script again to refresh my memory. When I was in elementary school, my parents took Carlos and I to a touring production of this play. Even at such a young age, I remember being moved to tears, but I find that the story and words have taken on a whole new meaning for me now. There is so much here about living life to the fullest because we never know when our time will be up.

I've chosen some scenes to use for the auditions next week, and have devised a short writing activity for when Jonathan and I choose the cast. It comes from Emily's monologue in the final act where she's enumerating all the things that held meaning for her when she was alive.

*The town. Mama and Papa. Clocks ticking. Sunflowers. Food and coffee. Hot baths. Sleeping and waking up.*

If Jonathan agrees, I'll have them write their own short "Good-bye Soliloquy," to include the most important things that hold meaning for *them*. Of course, I'll have to do it myself as an example. A few weeks ago, I couldn't have done it, but now … even though it might bring me to tears, I know I can.

I'm surprised to feel myself coming back to life, back to myself. Maybe it's the fresh sea air. Maybe it's the fact that it's been so long since Marc died. It might even be the sudden, unexpected presence of Ryan in my life. Whatever it is, I can feel myself lightening up. I can feel myself beginning to breathe more easily. And there's a glimmer of joy in my heart that wasn't there a few weeks ago.

After meandering around the BackStage Costume Shop (which is more like a warehouse than a shop) for more than an hour, I've gotten some great ideas for costumes for the kids, but I'm holding off ordering the rentals until we know our cast members and their sizes.

Kit is great fun to hang out with; she's full of stories about her life "on the road" back in her "younger days" when she was modeling. We eat a late lunch at the Broadway Deli on Maine Street in Brunswick, and Kit lights up a cigarette while I munch on a decadent brownie studded with walnuts. She drives us around her old neighborhood before handing me the keys to her Kia Soul (an appropriate car for such a spirited lady).

"Do you mind driving on the highway?" she asks as we approach her car. "I'm feeling a bit tired."

I easily agree because I love driving. On our way back to Seahaven, after several minutes of silence, Kit asks me how it's going with Ryan.

"It's going well," I murmur.

She reaches over and pats my knee with her still-youthful, ringless hand. Several colorful bracelets adorn her left wrist. "He's mighty cute, and very talented. Do you know where this is headed?"

I feel a surge of anger tinged with exasperation rising in my chest. "Headed? Why is everyone so interested in where this is headed? Why does it have to be headed somewhere?"

I keep my eyes on the road but out of the corner of my eye, I can see her eyebrows lifting.

"Sorry, dear. That was a poor choice of words. Let me ask something else. How are you feeling about him?"

"Oh." I loosen my shoulders a bit and my defenses settle down. "I feel good about him. He's … " I notice the stately pine trees guarding the highway. "He's good for me, Kit. I don't know how else to describe it. I know he's going back to New York when *Into the Woods* is over and I'll miss him, but it will be okay."

"Is this your first … relationship … since Marc?"

"Yes. And I know you're going to say that it's about time—"

"I'm saying nothing of the sort!" Kit holds her hands to her heart. "When Ollie died, suddenly time meant nothing to me. Your therapist has probably told you this, and you'll hear it more when you come back to TNA—everyone's timeline is different after any kind of a loss. It was four years after Ollie died before I even went on a date with a man, much less gave myself over to loving someone. My friend Cynthia started dating again five months after her husband died. Everyone is different, and when you're ready, you'll know it. Then again … some people are never ready, and that's okay too."

"Thanks for saying that. I do remember my therapist mentioning this once or twice." I glance at her and smile. She looks so calm and lovely, steady in her seat, silvery hair flowing past her shoulders like a magical mantle. I hope I'm as "together" as she is when I'm her age. I feel so comfortable with her; she reminds me of my mother even though they look nothing alike. "After Ollie, did you fall in love again?"

"Oh yes. Twice. The first time lasted six months before we both moved on. The second time was much longer. I was in my forties, still traveling a lot, doing photo shoots all over the world. It was quite a whirlwind. He was a photographer and we were often together on my gigs. André Dubois." She pushes her hair back and I sense that she is reliving a sweet memory.

"What happened?"

"We … grew apart. I decided to stop modeling and settle down in Seahaven about ten years ago and he couldn't do that."

"Couldn't?"

"Technically I guess the truth is that he *wouldn't* retire. He was such a free spirit, you see. There was something inside of him that made it so he needed to keep moving."

"That must have been painful."

She nods.

"Have you seen each other since?"

"Oh no. I made a clean break. I loved him, but I chose not to have an on-again, off-again relationship. That would have been much harder."

"Did you ever want to have children?"

I feel Kit glance at me. We're past Portland now, heading south toward Seahaven, and the sun is lowering in the west, streaking the sky with a pastel palette. "Ollie and I were planning for it, but you know how that story ended. Then I got so busy with my unexpected career and it never seemed to be the right time. Andre didn't want kids, and somewhere along the way I got used to letting go of that desire. I look upon Tess as I would a daughter; her children—Eva and Micah—are like grandchildren to me. I would do anything for them. What about you, Elena? Did you and Marc talk about having children?"

A leaden weight feels like it has landed in my stomach and I take a deep breath. It seems strange to me that only Camille and Carlos have ever asked me this. Not even Marc's mother has, and I'm glad for that because it always seemed too big to talk about. But now … here with Kit … I think I can let this story go. "Actually—"

At that moment, Kit lets out a disturbing moan. I turn my head briefly to look at her and am startled to see beads of perspiration on her forehead as her hands clutch her chest. Her face is as white as the art paste I saw in the supply closet at school last week. Almost as if I'm out of my body, I see myself grip the wheel tighter and steer us safely out of the right lane and onto the side of the highway. I slam on the brakes, fling off my seatbelt, and take her alarmingly cold hand in mine. Cars and trucks are flying by us. My heart is pounding so hard, I think it's going to break free from my body. Her pulse is thready, but I can definitely feel it beneath my trembling fingers.

Kit is unconscious but breathing. I fumble for the phone in my purse and press the emergency button for 911.

# Chapter 10

## KIT GILMORE

*"Katharine Gilmore? Katharine?* Can you hear me?"

Kit heard her name called again and tried to open her eyes. She'd been dreaming about her parents and Ollie. Beloved Ollie. He had been laughing and dancing with her just now … in the dream.

"Katharine Marie Gilmore! Can you hear me?" A female voice, low-pitched and gruff, pierced through the happiness of her dream.

Kit struggled to open her eyes. Yes, she had been dreaming, but who was talking to her now? It must be her mother. Jane Gilmore had always insisted on calling her only daughter Katharine instead of Kit. But … no. It couldn't be her. Even though Jane had been gone so long, Kit would recognize her voice anywhere.

A warm hand rested firmly on her shoulder but she didn't recognize the touch. What was happening? Why couldn't she open her eyes? She'd been dreaming about Ollie and … Another voice broke through the haze. She recognized this one. "Aunt Kit? Please wake up!"

Her niece. Dear Tess.

The potent blend of love and familiarity that echoed through Kit's body at the sound of Tess's voice surged through her spirit and enabled her eyes to slowly open. Tess was gazing down at her, hands clasped as if in prayer, long brown hair held back with a flowery headband. Luca, Tess's fiancé, also came slowly into focus. He was standing behind Tess, sending hands resting on her shoulders. But what were they doing here? And why was she in this weird bed, in this strange beige room with no window? Kit tried to lift her finger to rub the grit out of her eyes but the two tubes attached to her hand made it impossible.

Kit squinted at a middle-aged woman in a nurse's uniform who stood on the other side of the bed fiddling with a machine that was beeping rhythmically. "Welcome back, Ms. Gilmore. I'm Nurse Wanda. They call me Wanda the Wonderful." Tess and Luca chuckled; Kit looked puzzled. "You gave us all quite a scare."

Kit frowned, then turned her head back to her niece. "I don't understand. What is happening?" She hardly recognized her own voice, hoarse as it was.

"You're at York Hospital in Wells," Tess replied, bending down to kiss Kit on the forehead. "You've had a minor heart attack."

"Do you remember anything at all?" Luca moved to the foot of the bed, lifted the sheet, and gently rubbed Kit's feet through a dull gray pair of hospital-issue socks.

"I was … " Kit swallowed hard and started to cough. The nurse quickly moved a plastic cup and straw to her lips. The water seemed to revive her, and her focus cleared a bit as her dream of Ollie slowly receded. "Yes, Elena and I were driving … back from the theatrical supply store in Brunswick. She wanted costumes for—" Kit's eyes widened, remembering. "I must have passed out. Oh, my goodness, what about Elena? Is she all right? I'll never forgive myself if—"

Tess stroked Kit's arm. "Elena is fine. She's filling out the police report and will be here soon. Right now, all you need to think about is resting and doing exactly what Wonderful Wanda tells you to do."

Kit gazed away from the concerned trio gathered at her bedside and studied the bare boring wall as if it had important words inscribed on it. *A heart attack.* How was that possible? She was as healthy as a horse, or so Dr. Cavanagh had told her at her last physical. Kit meditated, walked miles every day outdoors. She practiced yoga, had massages, ate healthy, kept her body at a natural weight. Yes, she smoked, but not that much anymore. Oh, dear. Maybe the smoking is what caused this. Dr. Cavanagh had been suggesting that she quit ever since she moved to Seahaven. But maybe it wasn't the cigarette habit. What if she had the same heart defect that killed Ollie? She groaned, but not from physical pain this time. Kit was remembering all over again, after forty-four years, that her beloved Ollie was gone.

"You'll need to leave now," Wanda the Wonderful gestured to Tess and Luca. "Visiting hours start up again tomorrow at ten."

"All right," Tess said, reaching down to stroke Kit's arm. "We'll be back tomorrow. I love you, Aunt Kit."

Kit's eyes filled with tears as she felt the steady, pure love of her niece flow through her, skin to skin. "Thank you."

"I already called David and Samantha at Coastal Soul. They'll be covering for you the next few days, so don't worry about a thing. Oh, and I also called Marshall."

"Marshall?" Kit's heart gave a little flutter and she couldn't tell if it was from this "minor heart attack" or something else entirely. "Why did you—"

Luca winked at her. "We know how he feels about you … "

"And how you feel about him," added Tess with a mischievous smile. "He's driving up tomorrow."

Kit's heart quieted. Marshall was coming. Ollie was forever-gone but Marshall would be here. Two good men. "Thank you," was all she could manage to say to her thoughtful niece.

Tess turned at the doorway and said to Wanda, "Do you know when Aunt Kit can go home?"

"Dr. Cavanagh will be in early tomorrow to check on her. If all looks good, he'll get her prescriptions ready and she'll be on her way. You're one tough cookie, Ms. Gilmore!" Wanda patted Kit's leg through the bumpy white hospital blanket and bustled out of the room behind Tess and Luca.

# Chapter 11

## ELENA

*I've been staying* late at school for *Our Town* rehearsals, then visiting Kit in her cottage for a bit, and spending time with Ryan later at night after most of his performances. Kit is doing much better and has been told to rest. She's calling it a mild heart "event," but the doctor called it angina. Thankfully, there's no need for surgery at this time. The doctors agree that medication will be enough, at least for now. Medication *and* quitting smoking, which isn't going to be an easy thing for her, I'm sure.

Tess and her daughter, Eva, are usually visiting when I get to Kit's cottage. I like Tess a lot. She's had heartaches of her own but is now the office manager at Pearly Whites Dental here in Seahaven and is in a good relationship with her first love, a great guy named Luca. I think he said he ran a fishing charter service. Tess's son, Micah, is in South Carolina, recovering from injuries sustained in an accident last month during Army Basic Training.

Am I tired? A little bit! But I'm enjoying being productive again, and directing the play is challenging me to access my creativity more than I have in a long time.

After much discussion, and two afternoons of auditions last week, Jonathan and I have cast the play. We've got a wonderful lead cast— Kalila Jones is playing Emily, and Benjamin Cho is our narrator. We found a place for everyone who came to the auditions even if they don't have a speaking role, and Jonathan has gathered a few teens who will be helping him create the set.

Bea Lively—her name suits her to a tee—calls me every few days to remind me about my promise to consider ushering at Sands of Time, but I think that will have to wait. My life feels quite full already, thank you very much!

I am settling in. The apartment is familiar to me now, and even though the space is smaller than the house I shared with Marc in Massachusetts, it feels comfortable and I've made it my own. Also, I finally found the emotional strength to make space at the back of my bedroom closet for the two boxes of Marc's things. This feels like progress! They are out of my direct line of sight now, and I'm not tripping over them every time I walk to the bathroom. I felt a little guilty at first, but I've forgiven myself because I know I'm not trying to remove him from my life. I mean, I've already let go of so much of our life together. A few boxes of his personal things can be a gentle reminder of who he was. Who we were.

I feel like I've been at Seahaven High for years instead of weeks. Jonathan and I are working really well as a team. We've both been avoiding his ex-fiancée, Linnea, although I have seen her in the cafeteria and teacher's lounge a few times. She's shorter than me, with the shiny shoulder-length blond hair that most women envy. Not me. I love my hair, and while it may not be as shiny as Linnea's, it's much longer and thicker. Besides, my hair reminds me of my mother, and I'll take all the memories of her I can get.

I wonder why I'm comparing myself to Linnea. I don't know anything about her except for the fact that she ditched Jonathan at the altar. I have no idea why someone would do that to such a great guy. Maybe it just wasn't meant to be.

Marc and I *were* meant to be, right from the very first moment we met at Boston University. I was a junior, he was starting his senior year. What were we doing in a Comparative Literature course together? I know why *I* was there—an education major with a minor in English. Makes total sense. Marc, however, was a business major. The only reason a business major would be taking a Comp Lit course would be if he loved to read. And he did! In fact, in the short time we were together, I think he read more than I did—I never would have thought that such a thing was possible. He was a voracious reader, and didn't merely go after the typical male subjects like true crime and history. He read everything—mysteries, memoirs, cookbooks, graphic novels, historical fiction, self-help … even some romantic women's fiction that I'd left lying around the house.

He was, in a few words, a man after my own heart. Literally. I had never believed in love at first sight, but as soon as he took the seat next to me that September afternoon nine years ago, all long limbs and surfer-blond hair, I took one look in his baby-blue eyes that were scrutinizing me with what I can only call *understanding*, and I fell in love. We started dating the next day and were together, supposedly forever … until almost two years ago when his time—our time—was up.

As Camille keeps reminding me, I know that Marc is still with me, in my heart and in my memories. To be honest, I've kind of gotten used to being without his physical presence. There are things I don't miss, of course. His inability to load the dishwasher correctly, for one thing. Another thing I hated is that he never cleaned the sink after he shaved. Ugh. And don't ask me about how he always wanted to talk—out loud—when we were watching a movie.

He had the strangest habit of listening to the same song over and over and *over* again. I'm not exaggerating! In the car. In the shower. In our kitchen. Not only that, he would sing along with his chosen artist—loudly—and believe me, even though Marc thought he was God's gift to the musical world, he was never going to make it even close to an *American Idol* audition. It drove me crazy.

They say there are five stages of grief: denial, anger, bargaining, depression, and acceptance … and I've been through all of them in the last two years. Several times over. The hardest was the anger. Why him? Why us? I couldn't see past the disorienting finality of our life together, the numbing sensation of my life in ruins. And always, running through each stage was depression. I had to take a three-month sabbatical from teaching because there were days I could not get out of bed. Carlos used vacation time from the Animal Clinic in Seahaven and stayed with me for a few weeks. I will always be grateful to him for that. Marc's mother, Vivian, reached out, but I couldn't bear the thought of witnessing her pain alongside mine. In hindsight, I realize that we might have been a comfort for each other, but my grief seemed to make me extremely self-centered, and rightly so.

Would I give anything right now to hear Marc sing—albeit badly—again? Yes, I would. If he were here, would I complain about the way he loads the dishwasher? Absolutely not. And would I happily clean the bathroom sink after he shaves, without making any snide comments? Yes.

But I've let go of those fantasies. Over the last several months, I've landed off and on in the final stage of grief known as acceptance, and I'm surprised to find that I'm starting to appreciate the feeling.

Yes, there were friends who called and texted after he died. Some of them sent cards, and a few dropped off food. But they were in their own grief, I suppose. When I didn't return their calls, they didn't keep in touch. I understand now; it can be hard to know what to say to a young, grieving widow. The people I'm getting to know in Seahaven—Kit, Tess, Bea, Jonathan, and a few teachers at the high school—seem to like me for *me*, and not because I'm half of a couple that fits in with their lifestyle. Hopefully, our friendships will last longer.

Now of course, there's Ryan. We spend as much time as possible together during his breaks from the show. Yes, he's on the phone with his agent frequently, and has several auditions already scheduled for when he returns to New York in two weeks. He's obviously excited about the possibilities that await him; a few of the auditions are for major Broadway roles. I'm happy for him, sure, and I'm also going to miss him when he leaves.

I'm already planning a special good-bye dinner for him after the last show, two Sunday afternoons from now. I'm going to take him to Chloe's by the Sea and we're going to guess the secret ingredient in Chloe's Secret! The mother of Maggie Bessima, one of my students, works at Chloe's and she mentioned the other day at rehearsal that the next two Sundays are when "Chloe's Secret" will be on the menu. It's nice to have a secret informant! Ryan has traveled more than I have, and has eaten a greater variety of food, so he's hopeful that he'll be able to guess the secret ingredient correctly. After dinner, we'll have one more night together and he'll drive back to the city in the morning.

I admit it—I'm going to miss him, but it's not like we're in love. We're not "meant to be" for the long haul, but I am grateful that our paths crossed this fall. He's brought something out in me that I wasn't sure I'd ever feel again.

And he still reminds me of someone … someone from my past, but I can't figure out who it is.

The read-through of *Our Town* last week went great, so on Monday the following week, Jonathan and I gather the cast for our first attempt at staging. I should say, *my* first attempt. Jonathan stays for my pep talk and adds a few words of inspiration, then heads backstage with his team of four adolescent boys and one girl who all exude the same nerdy-techy vibe that Jonathan gives off. I can tell they're excited to be in "Mr. Mac's" presence.

While I'm explaining where and how I want the actors in the first scene to move, Ryan bursts into the auditorium, jogs down the center aisle, and leaps onto the stage.

"Hey, Elena!" He gives me a one-armed hug while kissing my temple. A few of the boys hoot and whistle. "Hey everybody! I'm Ryan Summers. If you've seen *Into the Woods* over at Sands of Time, you'll know me as Jack!"

The students break into lively chatter and a few of them call out how much they liked the show. I pull Ryan over to stage left, and we stand slightly behind the heavy burgundy velvet curtain. "What are you doing here?" I whisper.

He looks amused. "I'm here to help, remember? It's Monday, there's no show tonight. I can stay as long as you need me!"

Ah yes, I remember now. He said he was going to help with the scenery. "Okay," I reply, dragging out the word in order to buy myself more time. "Mr. Mac … I mean, Jonathan, is back stage right now with his team. He's already got a design mapped out and they're ready to—"

Ryan cracks his knuckles as he glances at the students onstage and those in the front row of the audience who are waiting their turn. They've all quieted down now and I've no doubt they can hear us. This heavy curtain is only partially hiding us and it's not soundproof. "No prob! I'll go back there and see how I can help. Ciao!" He gives a cheerful wave and continues around to the back where I can hear Jonathan explaining the details of his design. I've already heard his plan, which—to my delight—is simple and concise.

We begin rehearsal again but about ten minutes into the first scene, I hear a commotion backstage. "Take five, everyone," I say uneasily. Taking a break so soon is not the best idea, but I need to see what's going on.

The kids disperse and I make my way to the full-length burgundy curtain that stretches the width of the entire back of the stage. I find a break in the curtain and cautiously peek between its smooth edges. Ryan is gesturing widely, his back to me, as he emphatically—and quite loudly—explains his "vision" for the *Our Town* set, which doesn't sound simple or concise at all. I pause and look at the others. The kids are sitting around a small table, paying attention to Ryan but occasionally stealing glances at their teacher. Jonathan is standing with his arms crossed, sternly gazing at the younger man. I can tell that Ryan's dramatic presentation is having zero effect on him. I'm not sure if I should interrupt or if they can handle this on their own, so I wait, peeking around the curtain, listening intently. No one has sensed my presence.

I'm impressed that Jonathan doesn't interrupt Ryan. His steadiness in the face of this disruption—to his meeting with his team and to his well-laid plans—is calming. When Ryan pauses to take a breath, Jonathan steps a little closer and shakes his hand. Also impressive, especially since I've twice refused Jonathan's offer of a date, and he knows that I'm seeing Ryan.

"Nice to have you with us," he says quietly. "You've got some good ideas, very creative! But the team and I already have a plan worked out and we're about ready to start building the backdrop." He gestures to the students and they nod in agreement. "I've contacted Seahaven Hardware and they're about to deliver the materials we asked for. Maybe you could lend a hand to help us unload?"

Ryan nods and looks around at the teens, then back at Jonathan. I think he's about to agree, but it seems he isn't quite ready to let go of his ideas for the set. He perches on the edge of the table and directs his pitch to the kids alone. "Wouldn't it be cool to set the play in modern time instead of back in the early 1900's?" They fidget and frown, looking doubtful. "The town could be Seahaven or somewhere cooler like Boston or New York! We could even include an arcade, and update the whole thing to include video games and smart phones and—"

"Look, Ryan," Jonathan interrupts Ryan with gentle authority. "We appreciate your ideas. Don't we, Team?" They nod tentatively, curious to see how this is going to play out. To their modest knowledge, no one has ever challenged their teacher before. "I really hate to dissuade you, but you need to keep in mind that this is a high school production. We're not heading to Broadway." He finally notices me and winks but Ryan doesn't turn around. "At least *I'm* not," he continues with a grin. "Some of the kids on that stage, well … you never know."

Ryan shrugs, looking disappointed. He taps his fingertips together. "I was hoping to offer something different."

"I hear you. Something different is always good, just maybe not *so* different for this particular play. You know, Elena—I mean, Ms. Jeffries—and I are incorporating the play into our classroom lessons. She's going at it from a literary perspective and I'm focusing on the historical, so we can't change the setting or the time period. Does that make sense?"

I'm impressed with how Jonathan is explaining the situation to Ryan. It's almost like he's talking to one of his students—calmly and with respect.

"Sure," Ryan replies, dragging out the word thoughtfully. Almost immediately, his dramatic stance is over and he claps his hands briskly, jumps to a standing position and salutes the team.

"Okay then. I'm glad to help with unloading the materials." Even though his back is to me, I can tell that he's smiling again because the teens are beaming bright smiles back at him. "Whatever you need."

"Thanks, man! And hey, maybe we can do something with your suggestions about the brighter paint colors. I was thinking drab, muted earth tones, but I like what you said about lightening things up a bit."

"That'd be cool." Ryan rubs his hands together as if he's won the lottery. "Where are we meeting the Seahaven Hardware truck?"

Crisis averted, I offer a short wave and a grateful smile to Jonathan who nods and grins back. Ryan and the team are still unaware that I witnessed that whole scene through the gap in the burgundy curtain.

The next evening I'm in the waiting room at Bright Side Animal Clinic. Jezebel is meekly meowing in her pink carrying case; it's time for her annual check-up and I'm as nervous as she is. I know she hates being somewhere with strange sounds and smells, but I swear it's harder for me because I can't explain any of it to her.

Leah St. James, the social worker who leads the Together Not Alone group, is also in the waiting area, although the carrying case that rests beside her is dark blue … and empty.

"Hi Elena," she greets me pleasantly enough, but her eyes look sad. "Who is this little one?" She crosses the room and crouches in front of my case.

"This is Jezebel. We're here for her yearly exam. She was a stray kitten that kept coming to my front porch right after Marc died."

"Ah, so she's probably around two years old?" Leah murmurs softly and I notice that Jezebel stops meowing at the sound of her voice. Or maybe it's her presence that soothes my distraught cat. Leah does have a quiet, calming energy about her.

"That's right." I'm moved that she remembers my story from the meeting earlier this month.

"What a comfort, am I right?" She sits on the bench next to Jezebel and gently pats the top of the case.

"You are," I reply, nodding as I remember exactly what a blessing Jez was, and still is. I don't think I could have gotten through these last two years without her. "What about you?" I ask, pointing to the empty case on the other side of the waiting area.

Leah sighs and feathers her fingers through short auburn hair that is tinged with a few strands of gray. "I'm here to pick up my cat, Buddy. He's been sick for a while and Dr. Brightman kept him overnight with a new medication he's trying. By the way, Sam—I mean, Dr. Brightman—is the best vet. Your little one is in good hands here." Her face brightens as she says the vet's name. I know she's divorced and I wonder if he's single too. "The whole staff … they really care."

"Glad to hear it. My brother Carlos works here."

"No way! Carlos Fuentes is your brother? He's the best!"

"He is, and I love him to pieces. He's the reason I moved to Seahaven. How long have you had Buddy?"

"Six years. Not long enough." Leah shakes her head and tears glisten in her eyes. "He's the love of my life. My husband left me last year after my cancer diagnosis—I think someone mentioned that at group when you were there—and Buddy's been with me through every step of both of those losses. I know his time is limited, and I'm trying to get used to the idea of letting him go. Just … not yet."

We're interrupted by a smiling woman with gingery-red curly hair pulled back in a long ponytail. She's holding a clipboard as she opens one of the exam room doors. "Ms. St. James? Dr. B and Buddy are ready for you!"

"Thanks Carolina," Leah says eagerly, rushing over to where she was sitting and picking up the empty case. She turns to me before entering the exam room. "It was good to see you, Elena. You'll come again to TNA, won't you?"

I nod affirmatively, remembering the calming effect that the welcoming circle of fellow grief-carriers had on me, along with the significance I gleaned from the bowl of colorful sea glass. "I will, but I don't think I'll have anything new to share."

It seems that I've spoken too soon. After arriving home and letting Jezebel out of her carrying case, I check my messages. Vivian Jeffries, Marc's mother, has left me a voicemail.

# Chapter 12

*"Elena, it's so* good to hear your voice." Vivian's words invoke fond memories of Sunday suppers at her house from the first month that Marc and I met. She was a good mother-in-law, always ready to share a recipe or lend an empathetic ear. Vivian, a single mom to an only child, had a good career as a respiratory therapist at Brigham and Women's Hospital in Boston. Marc's dad, an insurance broker, died when Marc was three. From then on, Vivian did an excellent job of supporting their little family of two—financially as well as emotionally.

"Hi, Vivian. I'm glad you called." This feels like the right thing to say.

She clears her throat. "I know we haven't talked for a long time, but I was wondering if you would meet me this weekend. I've been clearing out … " I hear her take a sharp breath. "… Marc's old room. I'm getting ready to sell the house."

"Really? You're moving?"

"I am. I've finally retired, and after Thanksgiving I'm moving to Florida to be near my sister. You remember Jeanette?"

"Yes, of course. She was Marc's favorite."

"And he was hers. Now, I'm clearing things out and I … I want to give you something."

This surprises me. I didn't think Marc had left anything behind after we got married and bought a house. In fact, I distinctly remember spending time in his childhood room, helping him box things up for the Salvation Army and the local homeless shelter. The things that he kept? They're in those two boxes in the back of my closet, along with some other treasured paraphernalia.

"Wow. Thank you, and congratulations on your retirement. I've moved too."

"You have? The house in Dorchester where Marc … where you and Marc … ?"

"I sold it this summer and moved to Seahaven, in Maine, where my brother lives. You remember Carlos, right? There was an opening in the English department at the high school here." Her silence speaks volumes. I wonder if she's beginning to cry. "I'm sorry. I should have told you."

"No, no. It's okay. Well. It's good for you to be making a new start. And for you to be near Carlos."

"It is." I take a moment to think. It's not even a two-hour drive to where she lives in Lexington. This might be my last chance to connect with her before she moves to Florida. Marc would want me to do this. "Listen, I can drive down on Saturday afternoon for a visit. Will that work?" There's so much I need to tell her and I have no idea how she's going to respond, but I'm beginning to realize that I can't avoid her forever. It's time for me to do this.

"Goodness, yes. That will be perfect. I'm really looking forward to seeing you, dear."

I wish I could say the same.

The next day, I leave the *Our Town* rehearsal in the capable hands of Gretchen Ramos, a student teacher who graciously volunteered to be our assistant director (without my even asking!). As I head to the TNA meeting at the Community Center, I realize that I haven't been here since my first day at Seahaven High. I'm keenly aware of how different my life is now, how different I feel. The wind off the ocean today is brisk and biting, a preview of what the late fall and winter months will be like. I'm already wearing my winter coat, but refuse to put on mittens or gloves until it gets below freezing.

The group has settled into their customary comfortable circle and I pause beside Leah on the way to an empty seat. She's wearing her social worker "uniform" of a knee-length tailored linen dress, this time with a pale-yellow sweater. I admire a multicolored starfish necklace at her throat as it catches the overhead fluorescent lights. "How's Buddy?" I whisper.

"A little better today. Thanks for asking!" Leah turns her attention to the circle. "Okay everyone, let's begin."

There's the usual round of introductions where we mention our current state of grief. Leah's, again, is the mastectomy, her divorce, and Buddy's illness. Others acknowledge their individual losses—the death of a sibling, an elderly parent with dementia, a friend in hospice.

When it's my turn to share, I simply say, "I'm Elena and my grief is the death of my husband Marc almost two years ago, and also… " I swallow hard. Can I really say this out loud to these strangers? I glance around the circle, noticing that the faces feel familiar. Maybe they aren't strangers after all. My eyes land on Leah who nods kindly. "… the death of our baby. I found out I was four weeks pregnant the day of Marc's accident and I was so excited to tell him. But he died and … I miscarried two weeks later."

There. I did it. There are tears in my eyes, but I feel the support of the group holding me upright. The pain isn't as scalding as it was at the beginning, but I understand from my talks with Camille that this loss—the loss of a child who didn't even have the privilege of being born—will always feel tender, like an ancient bruise on my heart.

When the brief round of introductions is over, Leah gestures to the bowl of sea glass resting on the table in the center of our circle. "Elena, would you like to share first?"

I take an oblong piece of cloudy green glass and return to my seat. "I didn't think I'd have something new to share today. It's only been a few weeks since I've been here, but … " The others nod, encouraging me to continue. I tell them about the call from Marc's mother. "I don't want to go, but she's moving far away and I'll probably never see her again."

"Why don't you want to go?" asks Bea from her seat to my right.

"I never … told her about the baby." I grip the sea glass tightly.

"Ah," says Leah, leaning forward, elbows on knees. "Do you think she would want to know?" There is no judgment in her voice, only compassion with a whisper of curiosity.

"I'm not sure," I reply, tasting the anguish that coats my throat. "I mean, what's the point of telling her about a grandchild that she'll never get to meet?"

The group's silence holds me in place, then is broken by a thin elderly man. His pure white hair is trimmed short and his white goatee makes him look like Don Quixote. "My stepdaughter miscarried many years ago, and I carry that little girl's spirit in my heart, even though I never got to meet her." He gazes at me with milky blue eyes. "They were going to name their child after me if it was a boy. Milo." He smiles. "But it was a girl, so they named her Mila, which is Spanish for *miracles*, even though she didn't live. What is your baby's name?"

I catch my breath. He is speaking in the present tense, acknowledging the existence of my child in the here and now, not the past tense as I've always thought of him. Yes, a boy. I smile at Milo in gratitude. "Marc and I were both into literature, you know?" I point to myself and shrug. "I'm an English teacher and he loved to read. If it was a girl, we were going to name her Lyra, from *The Golden Compass*, one of Marc's favorite stories. If it was a boy, his name would be Finn."

"And was it a boy or a girl?" Anna asks from her seat next to Leah.

"I don't know for sure because it was too soon," I say quietly, a lump in my throat. "But I have a feeling it was a boy, so his name was Finn."

"His name *is* Finn," Milo corrects me gently.

"Yes. His name is Finn. Finn Jeffries."

"Good name! I loved that young man from the TV show, *Glee*!" says Olivia who is on the other side of our circle. I remember that she is one of Kit's closest friends—Ollie's sister—who recently lost her mother.

I laugh outright. "Marc and I did love watching *Glee*, and you wouldn't believe how much he loved to sing along. But we didn't name him after the football player on *Glee*. Another of Marc's favorite books growing up was *The Adventures of Tom Sawyer*."

Milo claps his hands. "I suppose that you vetoed the name of Huckleberry?"

"You got it!" I'm laughing with the group now, surprised but glad that even in the face of verbalizing such a difficult loss, there can be the lightness of laughter.

Leah looks around the circle, gauging everyone's expressions. She fingers the starfish necklace nestled at her throat and directs her gaze back to me. "How do you feel about visiting Marc's mother now?"

"A little better. She said she has something to give me, but I don't know what it could be. I feel bad about not staying in touch with her after … everything." I pause, lightly turning the sea glass over and over in my hand, enjoying the smooth feel of the once-sharp edges. Perhaps my own sharp regret about pushing Vivian away has also been smoothed into something that doesn't hurt to touch. Perhaps Vivian has forgiven me for not including her in my grief, for not reaching out to her in hers. But will she forgive me when she finds out that I've withheld something so precious from her?

On the way home from the meeting, I stop by Kit's cottage and find her sipping tea at her kitchen table. She doesn't look much different from before the heart event … maybe a little thinner, a few pale smudges of dark under her eyes. The fresh smell of peppermint greets me as I take a seat across from her. I wonder if she chose peppermint today as a way to lift her spirits, because the aroma sure is lifting mine.

She smiles. "I'm happy to see you, Elena. Let me make you some tea."

"Okay, thanks." I slump back in the chair and watch as she rises, graceful as ever, to fill a yellow teakettle from the faucet.

"Tell me what's happening in your world." Kit sets the kettle on the stove and turns up the gas flame underneath it.

"I really just came to check on you. I was at the TNA meeting today and everyone was asking about you."

She perches on the kitchen chair, keeping an eye on the kettle. "I was planning to go but it seemed like my get up and go … got up and left." She chuckles, then folds her hands on the table. "I'm doing okay. Doctor Cavanagh says I can go back to work in a day or two."

"And the cigarettes?" I ask tentatively as the teakettle begins a rumble toward a shrill whistle.

Quickly turning off the flame and removing the kettle from the burner, she replies, a bit sorrowfully. "Out the window."

"Not literally?" I say with a teasing smile, hoping to elicit a laugh.

No laugh, but a definite smile. "Very funny." She opens the narrow cupboard to the right of the stove, displaying several colorful boxes of tea. "Would you like peppermint also?"

I nod. "Most definitely."

She carefully withdraws a tea bag, drops it into an orange mug and pours the steaming water over it. She sets the mug in front of me and we both breathe in the minty sweetness. "Ahhh … " She smiles again as she sits down. "Enjoy." Waving her hand at me and my tea, she continues. "Of course, I couldn't throw the cigarettes out the actual window, because they would still be out there, on the ground, and I could just go out and light one up."

"I assume there are no more cigarettes in the general vicinity?"

"Correct." Kit drinks her tea. "I never thought I could stop smoking cold turkey like this, but Dr. Cavanagh scared me. The whole heart event scared me." Setting the empty mug on the table with an emphatic *thud*, she says, "I didn't think I could, but I'm doing it. I've had a little chat with myself. Yes, that's right. I've had a talk with the part of me who thinks she needs a cigarette, and I've made myself clear." She points an elegant finger at me. "You should be glad, dear girl, that you never started."

"Addiction is a difficult thing to get through. Maybe there's a support group for that too?"

She considers me as I sip the tea, savoring the minty freshness on my lips. "I will have to ask the doc about that. Now, tell me what's happening with you?"

"There's quite a bit. Are you sure you're up for it?"

"Most definitely. Take my mind away from thoughts of nicotine for a while, please!" The lightness of her tone along with her inquisitive gaze, encourages me.

"You know about Marc and how he died, right?" She nods. I run my forefinger around the rim of my mug. "Well, what I haven't told anyone except for Carlos and my therapist, up until today, is that the day he died, I found out I was pregnant with our first child—"

"Oh, honey!" Kit reaches across the table and lays her hand over mine. I can tell she knows what's coming.

"I lost him two weeks later. Finn. His name was … His name is Finn."

We sit in silence and I appreciate the feeling of being held without words, without physical touch. It gives me time to realize how good it feels to talk about this. I squeeze Kit's hand and take a long swallow of tea before continuing. "Anyway, I talked about it at TNA today and everyone was very supportive."

"I would expect nothing less. How are you feeling now, having finally shared Finn with more people?"

"I feel good, but wait! There's more. Marc's mother emailed me yesterday. She wants us to get together this weekend because she has something to give me."

There's a pale green wispy cardigan that's been resting on the back of Kit's chair, and she lifts it up and around her shoulders, under her silvery hair. "Interesting. She lives in Massachusetts, I assume?" I nod. "How long has it been since you've seen her?"

I shove the mug away, lower my head and rub my forehead anxiously. "I haven't seen Vivian since the funeral. Almost two years ago."

Kit waits patiently, arms folded on top of the table.

"I couldn't do it. I couldn't go to her. She reached out to me several times but I was so angry, so sad, so … everything. A few weeks went by and I had made up my mind to call her, but then I lost the baby … I lost Finn. Part of me knew that I should tell her because he was her grandson, but I just couldn't bring myself to do it. I took a leave of absence from school, and Carlos came to stay with me for a while. Eventually, I got back to my life—very reluctantly, I might add—and never got around to telling her. I feel so guilty about it now. I don't know if she'll forgive me."

"It seems like she's already forgiven you, if she wants to see you again and has something to give you."

I shake my head and meet Kit's kind gaze. Her gray eyes have a gentle light filtering through them, like soft sunlight breaking through a cloudy sky. "I do think she's forgiven me for not grieving with her after Marc died, but I don't know if she can forgive me for not telling her about Finn… back then."

Kit nods and looks away, gazing out the bay window at the afternoon sky, a few leaves drifting down onto the autumn-carpeted lawn, a blue jay at the feeder. "I've never lost a baby, of course, but I do know something about grieving with my beloved Ollie's mother." She scoots her chair around the table so she's right next to me. "Lillian took me in after Ollie died. My family didn't understand what I was going through. Mom wanted me to go right back to school and just get over it." She shakes her head. "As if one simply gets over a loved one's death like that. And my dad … he tried his best to follow her lead."

"I'm sorry."

"It is what it is. I came to peace with it a long time ago. My point is that Lillian was Ollie's mother, and she was grieving even more than I was. She was his *mother*; she'd known him his entire life, much longer than me. I can't even imagine the depth of that kind of loss, but she took me in and that made the biggest difference on my own journey. In fact, I am eternally grateful for Lillian's guidance during that difficult time. If I had stayed in Brunswick with my parents, there is no way I would have woken up from the foggy haze of my grief. Or if I did, it would have taken me a lot longer."

"You're lucky," I say, wiping my eyes and drinking more tea to clear my dry throat. "I could have had that too, but I wasn't able to see it or I would have gone to Vivian."

"Yes, I was lucky. Some would say I was blessed," she replies, leaning back in her chair. "I have the feeling that Vivian understands why you needed to grieve alone when Marc died, which means she'll likely be open to forgiving you for the rest of the story. After all, she's reaching out to you. She wants to see you. She has a gift for you."

I nod slowly.

"Are you considering telling her about Finn?"

"Yes. Everyone at TNA seemed to think it's a good idea, and that I'll feel better once I do."

"And what do you think?"

"I'm not sure. I mean, I want to. I really want to, but I'm afraid that she'll be mad at me and I don't want to give Marc's mother reason to be angry."

"Ah, but that's the chance we take when we tell someone the truth, isn't it?" Kit raises her eyebrows and waits for a reply.

"I guess it is."

"It sounds like you've been thinking 'what if Vivian gets angry?' Could you try to change that thought to something like, 'what if Vivian is glad that I told her?'"

What she's saying makes perfect sense. My mind has been full of *what ifs* that are not of the positive variety. I feel a shift inside me toward hope when I try to imagine Vivian meeting my news with—not necessarily happiness—but perhaps acceptance. "Thanks, Kit, that helps a lot." I stand and carry my mug to the sink.

"I'm glad, dear." Kit joins me at the counter with her own mug and hugs me. "Even though you didn't grieve with Marc's mother when he died, the way I grieved with Ollie's mom, I wonder if it's not too late to grieve together now."

# Chapter 13

## KIT GILMORE

### FEBRUARY 1980

*Kit snuggled as* far down under the covers as she could. Not necessarily to keep warm, because Lillian Mattheson's house was quite comfortable. No, Kit was buried under a soft set of Laura Ashley flowered sheets, assorted cotton blankets and a heavy white down comforter because she was hiding. It had been a long, dark six weeks since Ollie had died. Christmas, New Year's, and her own twenty-first birthday had passed— unnoticed. Uncelebrated. This was not a time for celebration.

She was in Lillian's beach-themed guest room, right across the hall from Ollie's room. Perhaps others might say that she was staying across the hall from Ollie's *old* room, but it still smelled like him and everything of his was contained within those walls, exactly as he'd left it. Because of this, she was calling it *Ollie's room.* Present tense. His twin sister Olivia's room was next door, but Kit hadn't seen much of her since moving in four weeks ago. This was because, on arrival, Kit had dropped her suitcase in this unfamiliar room in the house where Ollie grew up, thrown a minimal amount of clothing into a few dresser drawers, climbed into bed, and pretty much stayed there.

There had been a big blow-up at her own house after Ollie's funeral when Kit had announced that she was taking a semester off from UMO. Jane couldn't seem to grasp the fact that her daughter could hardly remember her own name or get out of bed, much less tackle a new schedule of classes, professors, and the college activities … all without her beloved Ollie. She had told Kit in no uncertain terms that if she wasn't going back to school, she couldn't live under the Gilmore roof.

"You have to get back on your feet, Katharine," she had insisted, as if this was as simple as recovery from the flu. If Jane had been a bit more like Cher in the movie *Moonstruck*, she might have screeched "snap out of it" as she slapped Kit's face, but Jane was a far cry from Cher. And there was no snapping out of this.

Carson tried to reason with his wife, but she was like a beached whale forever stuck in the sand. Unyielding. Unmovable. Focused exclusively on herself. It was Carson who had called Lillian and asked if Kit might stay with her and Olivia in Seahaven for a few weeks.

Those few weeks had turned into a month and a half and Kit couldn't imagine leaving. She knew that her father was paying Lillian for food, which made her feel a little less guilty for taking up extra space in a home where grief was hiding in every corner. Not that she was eating much; her entire world was centered between this bedroom and the bathroom that accompanied it. Carson and Frank came to visit once a week, every Saturday afternoon. Their presence lifted her spirits, but Frank was full of stories about UMO, and Carson never knew exactly what to say, although she knew his heart was in the right place. As glad as she was to see them, it was always a relief when they drove away.

Lillian and Olivia looked in on her a few times each day, their own countenances bearing the weight of their loss. They brought nourishing food and drink and calm voices, but Kit was existing on small swallows of soup and tiny bites of toast. On Lillian's insistence, Kit reluctantly stood under the shower every few days, but even that was an effort, and she took no pleasure in the sweet lemon shampoo and conditioner that Lillian so thoughtfully provided.

When Lillian came into the guest room every Monday morning to change the sheets and do Kit's laundry, Kit slipped into a clean nightgown and curled up onto the window seat that looked out over Lillian's garden, now covered in a foot of snow. She could remember what the garden had looked like when she'd visited Ollie here in August—lush, green, full of fragrant red and pink roses, orange lilies, and black-eyed Susans. But now it was a heavy blanket of white that felt familiar. Stark. Blank. Cold. Exactly like Kit's heart.

Lillian would talk softly to Kit during those Monday mornings, and Kit could hear the acute sorrow etched through the grieving mother's voice. She responded to Lillian as best she could, which wasn't much, but Lillian seemed to understand. A few times, she unceremoniously got into bed beside Kit and they cried together, which was soothing. Also, exhausting. Although their experiences were unique—the loss of a fiancé is quite different from the loss of a son—Kit sensed that they were united in their sorrow. The man they both had loved, in different ways, was gone. Grief was the necessary response.

The day after Valentine's Day, Lillian knocked lightly on Kit's door and entered after hearing no response. Kit was lying flat on her back, light brown hair limp around her shoulders, staring at the ceiling. It was early afternoon; bright sunlight streamed through the window that was framed with plain blue curtains. Kit looked at her never-to-be-mother-in-law with dull eyes. Lillian was wearing jeans, a black turtleneck, and a heavy fisherman's knit sweater the color of sunflower petals. Her curly brown hair—so much like Ollie's—was tucked into a black ski cap, and her hazel eyes, also like Ollie's, were gazing at Kit with a stern intensity that Kit had never seen.

"Get up." Lillian stood beside the bed and pulled back the comforter and two blankets, leaving Kit covered with a lone cotton sheet.

"Is it time to make the bed already?" Kit's voice was hoarse.

"No, it is not!" Kit heard a new tone of forced cheerfulness in Lillian's voice. "It's time for you to get up. Come on, we're going for a walk. Olivia is out with friends, so it's just you and me."

Kit raised herself on her elbows, squinting at Lillian. What had become of the quiet, sad woman who previously had tiptoed around the guest room so as not to intrude? "A walk?"

Lillian nodded briskly and went to the wide oak bureau to the right of the window. She rummaged through two drawers and came back to the bed holding a dark blue sweater and a pair of gray sweat pants. "That's right. We are going for a walk." She drew the sheet off Kit and dropped the clothing on top of her. "Get dressed."

Kit didn't move. Her feelings were ricocheting frenetically between anger and intrigue. On one hand, she resented this intrusion into her spiraling sorrow; she had come to depend on the solitary shadows of her grief. The physical energy she once had was somewhere in the vicinity of non-existent; taking a walk in the cold February Maine sunshine sounded impossible. Still, she trusted Lillian in a way that she didn't trust her own mother, and this new side of Lillian was ratcheting up her curiosity.

"Now!" Lillian's command was firm but kind. She didn't leave the room until she saw Kit uncertainly pulling on the sweat pants.

"Where are we going exactly?" Kit asked as soon as they were in Lillian's Jeep. She was shivering despite the warm winter coat her father had brought on his first visit, along with the hat and mittens borrowed from Olivia's closet. The brisk winter air had startled her as soon as she'd left the comfort of the Mattheson house which was inland and close to the highway. Kit had lived through twenty winters in Maine, so she knew about frozen landscapes and bitter winds, but not leaving her room for six weeks had sheltered her into a sleepy forgetfulness. Eyes and lips stung by the cold, Kit pulled the coat's collar up around her ears.

"Sunrise Beach," is all that Lillian said for the rest of the ten-minute drive. In fact, she didn't say another word during the entire two mile walk up and down the frozen sand. Kit did her best to keep up with Lillian; for a short woman, she sure had long strides. Whenever Kit would fall behind, Lillian would stand and wait patiently for her to catch up. A few times, Lillian put her arm around Kit as they walked, but mostly they were on their own paths, engrossed in their own thoughts. A few hefty seagulls circled overhead and followed them for part of the walk, squawking their indignation that the women had no food to share.

The sea was at low tide, puny waves breaking a hundred feet offshore. Ordinarily, Kit loved walking the beach and had often come here with Ollie. They had both delighted in finding shells, unique stones, and sea glass. But today was different. Today she was alone. Correction: she wasn't alone. She was with Ollie's mother. But delight was a feeling she simply could not access.

Although Kit longed to be back in the safety of the Mattheson guest bedroom, with Ollie's room right across the hall, she found that a tiny part of her was appreciating the view—a pale blue winter sky halfway to gray, partially-frozen sand crunching beneath their feet, and the tall, faded grasses that divided the shore from the parking lot. It was possible that the world was welcoming her back. But a world without Ollie wasn't a world she wanted to be a part of.

Later that day, for the first time since arriving, Kit joined Lillian and Olivia at their kitchen table for a simple supper of roast chicken and butternut squash dashed with cinnamon. The talk was minimal, each woman acknowledging, with silence, the big step that Kit had taken that day.

Kit managed to eat a slice of chicken that was half the size of her hand, along with a few spoonfuls of the squash. She noticed Lillian and Olivia exchanging a satisfied glance, but the only satisfaction Kit experienced was the quelling of a stomach hunger that she hadn't felt in six weeks.

Early the next morning, Lillian knocked on Kit's door again. This time, no sunlight streamed through the windows; everything was winter-dark. "Time to get up, kiddo! We're going to watch the sunrise."

"Sunrise? Are you joking?" Kit had finally fallen into an exhausted sleep a few hours ago and had no desire to leave the cozy nest of her bed.

"No, I am not! Hop out of that bed right now and bundle up. We're leaving in five minutes." The strident urgency in Lillian's tone somehow managed to inspire Kit to move her sleepy body out of bed.

They sat in the Sunrise Beach parking lot in the muted darkness of a frigid Maine morning. The warmth of the Jeep's heater finally enabled them to undo the zippers on their winter coats. Neither woman spoke until the sky began to paint the horizon with a long ribbon of burnished gold.

"Would you like to get out and walk?" Lillian whispered, seemingly entranced by the expectancy of the sunrise. They could see several people already moving briskly on the sand, along with a few rowdy dogs who were darting to and fro in unabashed glee.

Kit shook her head. "No." Her voice was flat as she rested her head against the window and closed her eyes. She felt as though her sorrow was permanently etched on her face, like it was leaking from her heart for all the world to see. Another excellent reason to stay away from people. She didn't want to share this sorrow with others, or listen to the questions that might so easily come to people if they crossed her path:

"Are you okay?"

"Is something wrong?"

"Why are you so sad?"

*I am definitely not okay.*

*Yes, something is very wrong.*

*I'm sad because the love of my life is dead.*

Kit didn't mind the occasional presence of Lillian, Olivia, Frank, and her dad. They didn't ask questions because they already knew the answers. The women fully understood; the men tried their best to comprehend her tremendous loss, but Kit wasn't ready to share this aching emptiness with the world at large.

"Katharine Marie Gilmore." Lillian unbuckled her seatbelt, reached across the center console of the Jeep, and tugged gently on Kit's chin until she turned to face Lillian. "Listen to me, dear heart. The sun is going to keep coming up, day after day, and today … today we are here to greet that sun." She dropped her hand from Kit's face, purposely removed the mittens from both of their hands and held Kit's trembling hands in her own.

"Lillian, I don't want to—"

"I know. Believe me, I know." The older woman sighed and squeezed her eyes shut for a moment before directing her gaze back to Kit. "Listen to me. Yes, our Ollie, our beloved boy is gone, but we still have the privilege of another day, and another day, and another day after that. We need to ask ourselves, 'What are we going to do with each day that we are given?'"

"The days … don't exactly feel like gifts … " Kit's voice drifted off, unable to imagine considering it a gift to wake up to another new day without Ollie.

"Of course. They don't feel like gifts. Not now. Maybe not for a long time. You know, I've lost several loved ones in my life so far, including Ollie's father, and I've come to believe that we go on … not just because we should, but because there is something larger, something greater than we are, that invites us to continue, in spite of the pain, in spite of the heartache. Do you know what I mean?"

In that moment, Kit's heart felt a faint pulse of hope, distant but clear. She had loved going to church at Saint Brendan's every Sunday during her childhood, had relished the feeling of someone or something greater watching over her, guiding her. Her mind turned to the interfaith services that she and Ollie had attended at UMO's Drummond Chapel once a month—the community, the ritual, the music, the prayers. In the canyon of her recent grief, she had forgotten all of that. Or maybe it wasn't forgotten after all; maybe she had belligerently shoved it aside, hoping to forget. And now she was starting to remember.

Kit found herself wondering. *Is there really something greater that can show me how to lift myself out of the frozen sand of my own heart?*

"Do you know what I mean?" Lillian repeated.

"Maybe," she replied.

Lillian nodded. "Call it God, call it Spirit or Source … Whatever name you choose to give it, I believe that it wants us to carry the light of our loved ones into the world for them, since they can't do it for themselves anymore. And that, dear girl, is what helps me to go on, even without Ollie … Even without his father."

Kit felt a brief smile forming on her lips. The sun was lifting its pregnant belly into the ribbon of light on the horizon as it slowly shifted into varying shades of crimson and violet. It was like standing in a museum, viewing an impressive watercolor framed with thick swatches of bluish clouds that looked like Morse code. Perhaps the Universe was sending her a message. Although Kit had never studied Morse code, she imagined that the message might be akin to what Lillian was telling her now.

"I like the idea of carrying Ollie's light, but how do we do that, exactly?"

Lillian smiled at the slight lift in Kit's voice. "That's a good question. Let's think about Ollie for a minute." The sun was fully over the horizon now, so bright that she pulled down the Jeep's visor to block the glare. "He was light in heart, open to anything and everything. He could talk to anyone … "

"Yes! People were drawn to him. I always told him he could have been a priest … or a bartender."

Lillian chuckled.

"Perfect strangers on the street, waiters in a restaurant, the barista in the coffee shop … they would tell him personal things even when he didn't ask! He took it all in, but never let any of it weigh him down."

"He was always like that; even as a teenager, he loved people, found everyone fascinating." Lillian nodded. "And don't get me started on his wicked sense of humor."

"I know! Ollie always knew how to make me laugh. He did love a good pun." A warm wave of memory flooded her heart, and for a few moments, Kit felt like herself again for the first time since Christmas Eve. Talking about Ollie and remembering him with his mother spread a healing balm on her weary, bruised heart.

Taking off her knit cap, Lillian fluffed out her brown curls and turned down the heat that had been blasting through the air vents. "I think the way we can carry his light is to try to bring one or two of those qualities into our own life. For example, I sure as heck am not going to start telling jokes; that's not my style. But I can pay more attention to people. I can listen harder to the server at the restaurant, the barista at the coffee shop, the teenager who's bagging my groceries."

"I see," Kit replied thoughtfully. "I've always been an introvert, very protective of my heart. Ollie changed that a bit; I can see that now. I won't be telling jokes either, but maybe I can carry his light by opening myself a bit more to people, to the world in general. He was especially passionate about at-risk teens. Remember our work at Preble Street Teen Center in Portland?"

"I do. He talked about it a lot, and he loved doing it with you. It was good work that the two of you did."

"Maybe I can find a way to continue to work with at-risk kids, to support organizations that help them."

"That's the idea! Remember the something greater than us that I talked about before? I call it Spirit, and I happen to believe that Spirit is still with us even in the darkest depths of our grief. Maybe *especially* during those times." Lillian patted Kit on the knee and shifted the car into reverse. "If we can hang on to that certainty, it will be easier for us to get out of bed in the morning. Not *easy* by any means, but easier. A little bit easier every day."

Kit turned her head to look back at the sunrise as Lillian steered them homeward. "Thank you. I don't know how I would get through this without you."

Later that night, after another supper at the Mattheson kitchen table—a bit livelier this time—Kit found a dark green leather-bound journal on her freshly made bed. Lillian had written on the first page:

*To Kit, with love from Lillian*
*May we carry Ollie's light in our hearts always.*

Eyes watering with tears of gratitude, Kit made her first entry.

*Dear Ollie,*

*You are gone and I am still here. I am still breathing. I can't seem to stop. Every bone in my body aches with your absence. We had such brilliant plans and we were going to do it all together. But you're gone. Forever. Now and then I can grasp this fact, but then an hour passes and it all seems so unreal again.*

*I don't know how I would be getting through this without your amazing mom. Lillian is grieving even more than I am. She's known you a lot longer, after all. But even though she's so sad, she is taking the time to care for me. My own mother wanted me to go right back to school but I couldn't do that, and then Lillian said I could stay here for a while. I DO want to go back to college, just not yet. It doesn't feel right somehow. I'm going to give myself some time to try to figure out how to live without you.*

*Your house feels more like home to me than my own home in Brunswick does right now. This is where I feel closest to you, so this is where I'm staying for a while.*

*This morning your mom made me get up IN THE DARK and we drove to Sunrise Beach. As the sun rose (why didn't we ever watch the sunrise together, Ollie?) she reminded me about Spirit. Remember those interfaith services we went to at school? I had pushed all of that away after you died.*

*Oh, and remember the service project that we joined for at-risk teens in Portland? That was special, doing that work with you. Anyway, talking with your mom this morning (God, it was so EARLY!), I was able to remember something I'd forgotten in the haze of this overwhelming grief. I remembered that we're not supposed to walk this life alone, and when I realized that, I suddenly understood that we don't die alone either. This comforts me so much when I think of you dying in your sleep on the morning of Christmas Eve. You were alone in your bed when you died, but you were never alone, not really.*

*The engagement ring you gave me is still on my left ring finger and I don't think I will ever take it off because in my heart, our love will always tie us together. We are each other's first loves. We are so lucky that we found each other when we did.*

*I'm going to find a way to continue to work with at-risk kids because I know that was important to you. And I will, eventually, open my heart again, and find more ways to carry your beautiful light into the world. It's going to take some time, but the sunrise each day will remind me of your light.*

*All my love, today and always,*
*Your Kit*

# Chapter 14

## ELENA

*I am understandably* distracted at the next two *Our Town* rehearsals. My stomach flops into knots every time I think of seeing Marc's mother on Saturday. Kit has told me how Lillian, Ollie's mother, helped her to grieve after Ollie died, and a bit about why the daily sunrise is so important to her. Now I'm feeling hopeful—albeit nervous—about spending time with Vivian this weekend.

Jonathan asks me a few times at rehearsal if I'm okay. There isn't time to tell him about Vivian, or the baby, so I brush him off. We're working so well together; I don't want anything to get in the way of our teamwork or the progress of the play. Gretchen, my new assistant director, is incredibly helpful and has taken over the duty of gathering props, so that's one less thing on Jonathan's plate. I've gotten the students' clothing sizes and rented all the costumes. One of the senior girls has agreed to do the stage make-up with Kit, so that's another load off my mind. It's my first year here and I want to make Mrs. Patterson, and the whole school, proud. Things are coming together, slowly but surely.

Ryan has been appearing at rehearsals sporadically this week. He seems to be getting along with Jonathan, although he's assisting me with stage direction more than he's helping backstage with the scenery. I'm not surprised to discover that he's as good at directing as he is at acting. The kids give him their undivided attention whenever he speaks, and I am grateful for this because it means I can slack off a bit. There are two more weeks of *Into the Woods* performances at Sands of Time Theatre, and then Ryan will be gone. I'm aware that my time with him is precious—woven with laughter, occasional lighthearted lovemaking, and eager conversation. His effervescent personality and ability to make people feel at home still reminds me of someone, but I can't for the life of me think of who it might be.

When the first week of October arrives, I begin wearing slacks and sweaters to work instead of skirts and short-sleeved tops. Autumn in Maine is nothing short of extraordinary. The leaves are turning brilliant shades of copper and crimson, etching stunning silhouettes against cool blue skies.

As I drive to Lexington on Saturday, the scenery is equally picturesque; I see autumn-stroked trees doing their best to brighten up a sky full of accumulating gray clouds. I am gathering up my courage with every mile, furtively attempting to brighten my previous "what if" thoughts into more hopeful ones. I glance at the passenger seat, which holds my purse and a plain brown envelope. "Finn," I say aloud with a nod to the envelope. "You're about to meet your grandmother." Hard as it may be, I know that this is what Marc would have wanted. I know that it's the right thing to do. Whatever the outcome.

Vivian is waiting for me at the door and her welcome is unabashedly warm. She hugs me for a long time, and I find her Shalimar perfume a comforting reminder of times gone by.

Sunday suppers with her and Marc. Walks around the neighborhood in December to see the Christmas lights. Occasional outings to Boston to see a show, attend an art gallery opening, or visit a museum. When Vivian lets me go, she leads the way through the spacious foyer into her warm living room. The furniture is the same as the last time I was here, but the built-in walnut bookshelves have been emptied and there are several large cartons lined up under the wide bay windows. I remember all those books and how Marc claimed to have read every single one. I wouldn't want to be the movers who will be lifting all those boxes.

Vivian stands beside me, her arm around my waist as if she can't quite let me go. "Would you like some coffee or tea? There's a fresh pot of each ready. Oh, and I made those snickerdoodle cookies that you used to like."

My heart softens as I study her blue eyes that are so like Marc's. I wonder if Finn would have had the same eyes. "Some tea and a cookie would be nice, thanks." I settle myself on the familiar sofa while she hurries into the kitchen. Clutching one of the brown and gold paisley cushions to my chest, I look around the living room. It seems like Vivian has already packed many of her things away. There used to be a dozen or more framed photos on the mantle over the fireplace and now there is one lone picture that shows her and Marc dancing at our wedding. They are looking at each other with such love; I blink back tears and remember what an amazing day it was. I will always remember how he smiled at me during our first dance, and the sexy endearments we whispered in each other's ears.

"Here you go!" Vivian sets a mug painted with cheerful daisies on the small table beside me, along with a matching plate of cookies. Her hair is grayer and shorter than the last time I saw her. She used to be naturally blond, just like her son. She's still tall and slender, though, and she moves with equal measures of caution and grace.

I bite into the sugary cinnamon cookie. "This is so good, Vivian. You always made the best cookies."

She settles one cushion away from me on the sofa and angles her body so we're facing each other. "You can still call me Mom, dear. I mean, if you want to." Her voice is a little shaky and I realize that she's as nervous as I am. She had urged me to call her "Mom" from the first time we met, and I gladly did so; Vivian exuded a maternal nurturing vibe that I sorely missed. I had often wondered if my own mother—from beyond the grave—was somehow able to orchestrate my meeting with Marc in order to provide a mother figure for me. I have always thought of Vivian as an added bonus that made Marc's love all the sweeter.

"All right, *Mom*," I tease. "These are really, *really* good."

"I'm glad." She folds her fingers into fists, then shakes them out and looks down. "I haven't made them in a long time."

I brush the crumbs from my hands and take a sip of tea. "Well, I'm glad you made them for me."

Vivian looks down at her fidgety hands as I look around the living room, not sure where to begin. My students would label this moment with one of their favorite words—*awkward*! As I stare at the earth-toned patterned drapes and color-coordinated textured wallpaper, I'm aware that this is so uncomfortable because the one person who always brought us together is not here. Vivian and I never had the opportunity to create a relationship separate from Marc. He was always with us, and that was exactly how we all wanted it to be.

As my gaze falls on the large brown envelope that I've tucked under my purse, I suddenly realize something important. There is another being who can bring us together now.

I pick up the envelope and hand it to Vivian with a tentative smile. "This is for you."

She takes it from me and holds it gingerly on her lap. "Is this something of Marc's?"

"You could say that." She's probably thinking it's something that he wrote or a photo of him that she's never seen.

I watch intently as she opens the unsealed flap and pulls out a large sheet of black and white film. She holds it close to her face, scrutinizing the details. "Is this a … sonogram?" I nod. "And what does it say at the bottom here?" She points to the typed lettering under the image. "I don't have my glasses."

"It says Baby Jeffries."

Vivian drops the sonogram in her lap and stares at me. "I don't understand. How on earth … ?" Her voice trails off as she picks up the image and studies it again. "Is this Marc's baby? Did you—"

I interrupt before her confusion takes over. "Yes, I was carrying his baby. But I miscarried a few weeks after he died. He never knew. I was going to tell him, that night, but … " I swallow hard and rub my cold hands together. "I'm sorry I never told you. So sorry. It was all too much. I couldn't bear to … " I glance up at her; she's staring at me with a look in her eyes that I can't decipher. "I'm sorry that I wasn't there for you. I wasn't … I couldn't … "

She picks up the film again and holds it to her heart. I watch uncertainly as she stands and walks slowly out of the room, head bent, a few tears etched on her pale cheeks. She seems to have aged ten years in the last ten seconds.

Distraught, I take another sip of tea, wipe my sweaty palms on my jeans and begin pacing the living room. I can hear Vivian quietly crying in another room, so I follow the sound and find her in the kitchen. Her hands grip the edge of the white marble counter that sits in front of a wide window bordered with red checkered curtains. The sonogram rests upright in the dish drainer to the right of the sink.

"I didn't know," she whispers again and again. I can feel her pain reverberating through my own body.

Standing behind her and rubbing her shoulders, I say as gently as I can, "Mom, I am so sorry. I should have told you." She turns to me then and I open my arms to her. We cry together for the first time since Marc died, vacating his side of our unique family triangle. I know that we have each cried copious tears in the individual confinement of our loneliness, but crying together is healing in a way that I never expected.

Later, we sit on the sofa again. "Did I hear you say it was a boy?" Vivian blows her nose and tucks the tissue into the sleeve of her sweater.

"Yes. I mean, it was too early to know for sure, but I had a feeling … His name is Finn."

"Finn. Finn Jeffries. I like that. Marc always loved Huckleberry Finn from the Tom Sawyer books." Her eyes look brighter now and her body is more relaxed.

"He did. I had to steer him away from the name Huckleberry, though."

She bursts out laughing and I join her. "Can you imagine if I had to tell my sister and my friends that I have a grandson named Huckleberry? What a hoot!"

The rest of our visit goes more smoothly. I tell her about my new school, *Our Town*, the TNA group, and Camille. For some reason that I can't quite identify, I choose not to mention Ryan. Vivian livens up the room with stories about her retirement party, the autistic boy down the street who has been doing yard work for her, and the new condo she's buying in Florida near her sister. Before I leave, she pulls out a burgundy leather photo album from the bottom shelf of the coffee table. "I want you to have this."

Curious, I open the thick cover and discover a colorful scrapbook dedicated to Marc Christopher Jeffries. As I turn the pages, I see baby photos of my former husband, then photos of him in elementary school with longer hair and a few front teeth missing. I see the young man he became in middle school and high school. Graduation. Prom. After that there's a series of photos of Marc as an adult. Marc alone. Marc with me. Marc with me and Vivian. At the last page, I look up at her in wonder. "You made this for me?"

"I did. Don't worry, I kept plenty of photos for my own scrapbook. Do you like it?"

"I do. And I'll treasure it always." I reach over and kiss her on the cheek. "I have photos of us together but none of him growing up. Thank you, Mom."

Standing, she picks up the sonogram—one of only two pictures we'll ever have of Finn—and carries it reverently to the mantle. It finds its place, right where it should be, next to the picture of her with Marc on our wedding day.

That night, at home, I am emotionally exhausted from my time with Vivian. Who knew being so truthful could be so draining? I take a quick shower before heading out to see *Into the Woods* one more time before it closes next weekend. Ryan has secured two complimentary house seats, so I'm taking Carlos with me. In my car, I tell him about the drive to Lexington that afternoon. "I told her, Carlos. I told Vivian about the baby … about Finn."

"Elena, I'm so proud of you!" He turns in his seat to better see my face. "I can't imagine what that was like."

"It was hard at first, but eventually … it was better than okay. I told the TNA group this week too."

"My word, girl! Life in Seahaven must agree with you. You've come a long way in the last month."

I nod, steering us off Route 1 and into the already-crowded Sands of Time parking lot. "I do like it here. You probably wish I'd moved sooner."

He shrugs, releasing his seat belt once we're securely parked. "Maybe I do, but it had to happen in its own time. When you were ready."

I laugh and open the car door. "I wasn't exactly ready, dear brother, but I moved here anyway."

"Because the time was right," he adds, taking my arm and leading me into the theatre.

The performance revives me; I'm once again immersed in the magic of live theatre. Particularly Ryan's character—Jack—who grows from a naive little boy to a brave young man who fights giants and grapples with the untimely death of his mother. Carlos hands me a tissue near the end when my heart aches for the four characters—Cinderella, the Baker, Jack, and Little Red Riding Hood—who have been left behind.

Later, in my apartment, Ryan chatters away eagerly about the show, the friends he's made, and a few new opportunities that are on the horizon for him.

"You'll come see me in New York, right?" He tugs at my sweater and pulls me down next to him on the sofa. I lean into him, admiring the tautness of his body and his clean citrusy smell. He must have eaten an orange after the show.

"Of course," I reply automatically, but I wonder. Will I? Part of me wishes this could continue; I find him equal parts comforting and enlivening. But another part of me knows that what we're experiencing together is fleeting and fragile, built on nothing but time and circumstance, which is not the best foundation for a lasting relationship. I wonder if Ryan has grasped this yet, or if he is thinking that we can make this work after he leaves.

We lapse into silence. It's highly unusual for Ryan to be quiet for this long, but I'm enjoying the lull. "What did you do today?" he finally asks, "while I was slaving away on stage for two performances?" He flashes a mischievous grin but I know he's teasing; Ryan lives to be onstage.

I hesitate, then sit up and push my hair over one shoulder. How much should I tell him? How much does he need to know? "I went to visit Marc's mother in Massachusetts."

"Cool." He gazes at me with curiosity. "Do you see her often?"

"This was the first time since the funeral."

"Huh." He draws his body up so he's on the edge of the couch next to me, our thighs touching. "I take it you two weren't close."

"We were. Before." I move a few inches away from him. "It was so hard, you know? I wasn't myself after I lost the … I mean, after Marc died. I know I should have reached out to her but—"

"You had to take care of yourself first."

His perceptive response calms me. "Yes." I feel no need to explain further and he doesn't ask any more questions.

"You're a strong woman, Elena Jeffries." Ryan stands, grabs my hands in his and leads me into a quick waltz around the room, even though no music is playing. Jezebel watches sleepily from the blue chenille pillow on what was once my mother's favorite rocking chair. "I've never known anyone like you," he whispers in my ear and I find myself relaxing into the dance.

I've never known anyone like him either.

Or have I?

# Chapter 15

*It's the following* Sunday after the last *Into the Woods* performance, and I'm standing in front of Chloe's by the Sea, waiting for Ryan. I glance at my phone. He is now officially ten minutes late and I don't know how long they'll hold our reservation. I'm pulling my coat tighter around me because it's chilly tonight, when my phone chimes with a text.

*Sorry can't make it. Important audition first thing tomorrow in NY. Need to hit the road now. Will try to make it back for Our Town opening night. Take care.*

The kids will be disappointed if Ryan can't make it back for their show. They've come to love his brisk energy and lively stories. He makes them laugh. Heck, he makes *me* laugh. Or I guess I should say, he *made* me laugh. My heart feels weary and lonely for the first time since Bea introduced us after that dress rehearsal. Was that only a month ago? I sigh as I pocket my phone without replying.

I wish he had come by the restaurant to say good-bye. The sharp twist of disappointment that flares up in my heart is small and useless; it flickers out as soon as it rises. I knew Ryan was leaving tomorrow but I'd been looking forward to one more night with him. Am I disappointed? Yes. But I find that I can hold my unhappiness gently while I take a breath and let him go. It's time to move on with my life here in Seahaven. Halloween is coming, along with something called The Great Big Seahaven Halloween Scavenger Hunt. I have no idea how that's going to play out exactly, but it sure sounds like fun.

As I enter the restaurant to cancel the reservation, I see Kit with a few others at the hostess stand. As soon as Kit sees me, she gives me an enthusiastic hug and introduces me to Marshall Sorenson, her former agent and now "beau" as she tenderly refers to him. Marshall is much taller than Kit, with clear blue eyes and a head of thick hair as silver as hers. He reminds me of a taller, leaner version of that handsome actor from *The West Wing*. What was his name? That's right, Martin Sheen. Kit's niece Tess is also here with Luca, both of whom I've seen at the hospital and in her cottage.

"Are you here for dinner?" Tess asks.

"I was, but … " I glance at Kit. "Ryan canceled last minute. We were going to try to guess Chloe's Secret."

"That's too bad," says Kit. "I know you were looking forward to it. Why don't you join us instead? We're here to discuss wedding plans. We can discuss the secret ingredient together."

"Wedding plans?" I say, raising my eyebrows at Kit and Marshall.

"No, not theirs. Not yet anyway," says Tess, putting her arm around Luca. "Ours."

"How exciting! But … I don't want to intrude."

"It's not an intrusion at all, Elena." Marshall smiles broadly and turns to the hostess. "We'll be a party of five instead of four."

After we're seated and everyone has ordered, I ask politely about Tess and Luca's plans. They'll be getting married in April, with the reception to follow here at Chloe's by the Sea. "It's going to be quite lovely," adds Kit, dipping a piece of sourdough bread into a small bowl filled with bright green olive oil.

The conversation moves to the roles that Tess's daughter, Eva, and Luca's son, Teo, will play in the ceremony. It brings back memories of my own wedding. Marc's niece and nephew were flower girl and ring bearer. Usually when these wedding memories arise, there are tears in my eyes, but today I have a smile on my face. Interesting.

When the server—a middle-aged woman wearing black slacks and a pristine white collared blouse with the name *Francine* embroidered on it—brings our meals, she sets "Chloe's Secret" in front of Marshall. "If you think you know what the special ingredient is, write it down on this piece of paper and I'll hand it over to Chloe in the kitchen."

"Can't you tell us?" Luca winks at Francine who hands the paper to Kit.

The server laughs loudly, claps a hand over her mouth and whispers dramatically, "Even *I* don't know what it is! Chloe. Tells. No. One." She smoothes her work-worn hands over her starched white apron. "Enjoy the meal."

We do enjoy the meal but we're all baffled by Marshall's food. It looks like a thick stew with lamb, potatoes, and a variety of colorful vegetables. He passes it around so we can all take a taste; it has a distinct foreign flavor and is unquestionably delicious. Marshall takes a sip of wine to "clear his palate" and tastes the concoction a few more times.

"By George, I know what it is!" he exclaims with delight. "Give me that piece of paper, dear." Kit hands him the paper and he scribbles a word, then holds it up for us to see. *Umami.*

"Good heavens, Marshall," says Kit, looking at him curiously. "I've never even heard of that!"

"Me either," Tess and Luca say at the same time.

As for me, I'm no expert in the kitchen, aside from some of my mom's Puerto Rican dishes. I probably haven't heard of half of what went into this amazing dish.

Marshall explains that umami is a savory seasoning in Asian recipes that is derived from seaweed, although he's not quite sure if this umami is the Asian kind, or a more widely known kind made from mushrooms. In a few minutes Francine is back, smiling broadly. "You got it right, and your meal, including dessert, is on the house, sir!"

She starts to leave, but he calls her back. "Isn't Chloe going to come out and congratulate us?" He sounds disappointed.

Francine turns back to us, frowning. "Chloe? Come out of the kitchen?" She shakes her head and glances over her shoulder as if to see if anyone is eavesdropping. "That has never happened and I've been working here since she opened last year." She shakes her head sternly in Marshall's direction. "Don't even ask."

He holds up his hands as if to end the conversation. "No worries. I was hoping I could meet her."

Francine rolls her eyes and shakes her head again. I can tell she's thinking that Marshall is completely clueless.

"That is mighty curious," he says after Francine has efficiently cleared our table and brought us coffee and tea. "I've never known a chef who wouldn't be delighted to come out from the kitchen and meet a satisfied guest. Do you know anything about Chloe?" He directs his question to Kit who shakes her head, then looks at the rest of us.

"Don't look at me," I say with a shrug. "I'm new in town." Tess and Luca are equally ignorant.

We're still discussing the mysterious Chloe when I notice Jonathan entering the restaurant with a woman. I sit up straighter and look more closely. It's Anna, from TNA, the one who explained the significance of sea glass to me at my first meeting. The one whose husband died of a heart attack earlier this year. I'm aware that I'm seeing Jonathan with a beautiful woman, that my breath has quickened and I'm feeling a slight pang somewhere in my chest.

Maybe I've had too much coffee today. Anna is old enough to be his mother. Isn't she?

As they are led to their table, Anna spots me and waves cheerily. She nudges Jonathan, hastily drops her purse and coat on a chair, then heads our way. Jonathan looks up to see where she's going and he breaks into a wide smile as he soon as he recognizes me. He takes off his jacket but doesn't sit down. I wonder if he's considering whether or not he should follow Anna.

"Elena!" Anna greets me by laying a lightly-freckled hand on my shoulder. "It's so good to see you!" She's wearing white woolen pants and an emerald green silk tunic with a chunky statement necklace that is made of tiny white shells and bits of multi-colored beads and sea glass. There's a large silver mermaid charm dangling from the end of it.

I introduce her to the others as Jonathan walks up and stands beside her. "I'm happy to meet everyone," Anna says. Her shoulder-length white-blond hair is tucked behind her ears; her ocean-blue eyes are wide and friendly. The tips of her fingernails are painted the same brilliant green as her tunic. "This is my nephew, Jonathan MacKenna."

I let out a breath I didn't know I was holding. Her nephew. Why am I so relieved that they aren't a couple? "Hi, Jonathan," I say, looking up at him. Familiar hazel eyes rimmed in gold smile back at me and hold my gaze. Words fly out of my brain faster than a missing homework excuse escapes a student's mouth.

The silence continues until I realize that everyone is looking at me strangely. "Elena?" Kit interrupts my reverie … or whatever was happening inside my head just now. "Do you and Jonathan know each other?"

"We … we do," I stammer, grasping my water glass as if it will tether me in place. "He's a history teacher at the high school."

"We're working on the senior class play together," he adds. "*Our Town.*"

"Oh, I love that play," says Tess. "I haven't seen it in a long time."

"I think there's a video of an older version," Luca replies. "We could rent it."

"Yes," adds Marshall, looking with curiosity between me and Jonathan. "There are several. I recommend the version where Paul Newman plays the Narrator."

"That's my favorite, too!" Jonathan replies. He looks at me. "I have the DVD. We should show it to the kids!"

"Sounds good," I say, finally taking a sip of water.

Anna studies Jonathan curiously for a moment, then directs her attention back to the others. "Would you mind if we steal Elena away so she can join us at our table?" I start to interrupt, but she continues. "I'd love it if you'd bring your coffee and keep us company. Jonathan and I are going to talk about the Seahaven Halloween Scavenger Hunt. It's October already, our favorite time of year."

Aunt Kit is trying to hide a smile. She waves me away and mouths the words, "Go, have fun!"

Do I have a choice? Yes, I guess I do. I can sit right here at this table and finish my coffee, then go home to my lonesome apartment and spend the night with Jezebel. Suddenly, that doesn't seem like the better choice. What will happen if I do join Anna and Jonathan? Maybe I'll get to know them better. Maybe I'll find out what this Seahaven Scavenger Hunt is all about; every time I hear someone talk about it or see one of the many posters scattered around town, it sounds more and more like fun. Maybe Anna and I can become friends. Maybe Jonathan and I will … wait! Where did that unfinished thought come from? And do I want to know the rest of it?

I stand quickly, hoping to steer my mind back to the present moment. "Sure, I'd like that." Surprisingly enough, I find that it's true.

Anna and Jonathan have secured a table by the window. From my seat, I have an excellent view of the sky darkening into an unassuming sunset. It rained earlier today and some thick clouds are still arrayed on the horizon, but the setting sun is leaving pale streaks of smoky plum and lavender. I wish I could paint the sky right now.

I tell them it's not too late to order Chloe's Secret and offer to share the mystery ingredient, but Denys, our server—a stocky young man with thick brown hair and a sprinkle of acne—overhears and wags his finger at me. "One winner per day, only," he says in a slightly foreign accent. "Old man already guessed it." He points at Marshall and Kit's table.

As apprehensive as I was about leaving my comfortable seat at the other table, I'm finding the conversation with Anna and Jonathan lively and interesting. I discover that Anna is a well-known children's author who writes a popular middle-grade series about mermaids. Her pen name is Anna M. French.

"I love mermaids," I say after they place their order and Denys refreshes my coffee. "And I see you're wearing one." I point to her necklace.

"Yes," she replies, touching the silvery mermaid adorned with sparkly blue and purple glass beads. "Jonathan gave this to me last year for Christmas."

"I did!" he exclaims, smiling back at her.

"He's an excellent gift giver."

"I learned from the best." They high five each other and I'm touched by how close they seem, how comfortable they are with each other.

"So, you're Anna's nephew," I say, looking directly at Jonathan. He's wearing a white cable knit sweater and dark jeans, quite a change from his regular school attire of dress shirts and ties. It looks good on him.

"My mother was her sister." He glances at Anna as she smoothes a flowered napkin onto her lap.

"Was?"

"Natalie died two years ago. She had an inoperable brain tumor that was causing seizures." Anna states this matter-of-factly, as if it had happened to someone else, but I can see the remnants of pain in her eyes.

"I'm so sorry. And your husband, too … That's a lot of loss in two years."

She nods and sips from a water goblet. "We're no strangers to loss, are we?"

"I appreciate what you shared at my first TNA meeting about the sea glass. It's been so helpful."

"Good!" Anna replies. "I've tried to get Jonathan to come to one of the meetings, but he seems okay." I nod, agreeing. He seems more than okay to me. "We all process loss and grief in different ways."

"I wasn't okay for a long time," Jonathan reminds Anna. He picks up his fork and points it at her. "Aunt Anna writes stories for kids about living with loss, from the points of view of different mermaids. She's famous for it, even goes around the country speaking at schools and parent-teacher meetings."

"Wow!" Everything about this woman is fascinating. "I'd love to know more about what mermaids have to do with loss. I don't quite see the connection."

Anna laughs, a lighthearted sound amongst the chatter of other diners and the murmuring ocean in the distance. "Basically, the idea springs from an ancient legend about a mermaid who fell in love with a human, a ship's captain. One night, when his ship was in a disastrous storm and about to capsize, the mermaid calmed the seas and righted the ship, even though she knew that

Neptune, King of the Ocean, had forbidden mermaids to change the laws of nature. The captain lived, but the mermaid was banished to the depths of the ocean where her tears turned to sea glass. Part of the legend says that the color of the tears a mermaid cries match the color of her tail, so each of my books reflects a different mermaid with a different color tail and therefore … different colored sea glass tears. I don't know what I'm going to do when I run out of colors!"

"That is fascinating," I reply. "I suppose you could write about a mermaid with a rainbow tail, or maybe there are mermaids with tales of combined colors? That could be fun."

Anna taps the side of her water glass and smiles at me. "I think you're onto something there." She reaches into her purse and jots something down in a small notebook, clicking her pen a few times thoughtfully before putting it all away. "Thank you!"

Jonathan leans toward me and shields his mouth with his hand as if he's telling me a big secret. "The M in Anna M. French actually stands for Margaret, but she tells the kids her middle name is Mermaid."

This makes me smile. Denys places a platter of rolls and sourdough bread on the table. Jonathan picks up a roll and immediately starts slathering it with butter. "Want one?" He nudges the plate in my direction.

"I'm completely full," I reply, patting my stomach. I suddenly realize that it's true in more ways than one.

Later, as we're leaving Chloe's, Anna heads to the ladies' room while Jonathan walks me to my car. I learned a few other things about him at dinner tonight. He's a board game fanatic. He also dresses up as the historical figures he's teaching about—Benjamin Franklin is his favorite. Another interesting thing about Jonathan is that he subscribes to the New York Times, Wall Street Journal, Portland Press Herald, and the Seahaven Citizen. These are the actual printed *newspapers*, not the online versions, which I find downright impressive since so many people—including me—get the news online these days. Right now, he's telling me that Halloween is his favorite holiday.

"Seriously?" I laugh, buttoning my coat and reaching into my purse for the car keys. "Not Christmas? Not your birthday? Thanksgiving even?"

"Nope. It's Halloween all the way! You heard us talking about the Great Big Scavenger Hunt, right? My parents are the ones who started it. Dad still heads up the steering committee. I was on that committee once, but it wasn't any fun because I knew ahead of time the list of items we were supposed to look for, so—"

"You couldn't actually participate."

"That's right! I lasted exactly one year on Dad's committee. Now it's more fun to be in the crowd." He looks at me thoughtfully. "Here's an idea. Maybe we could do the Scavenger Hunt together this year. Would you like that? Or will you be going with Ryan?"

Ryan. Between dinner with Kit's family, and spending time with Anna and Jonathan, I'd almost forgotten about Ryan. "*Into the Woods* ended today, so Ryan is heading back to New York. He might be able to come back for opening night of *Our Town*, but … for all intents and purposes, he's gone." I look into Jonathan's eyes with a smile that I feel to my very core. "I'd love to go with you to the Scavenger Hunt. It's the Saturday before Halloween, right?" I recognize a new tone in my voice that I haven't heard in a long time. This is what I used to sound like before Marc died—eager, excited, happy to have something to look forward to. How very, very interesting.

"That's right," he replies, and I can see how happy I've made him.

I also notice how happy I've just made myself. Saying yes to new things can do that to a person. Saying yes to new things is doing that to *this* person.

"See you in school tomorrow?" he asks.

I nod as Jonathan moves a step closer. Is he going to kiss me? I don't think I'm quite ready for that yet and feel relieved when he thinks better of it and steps back.

As Anna exits the front door of Chloe's, she waves good-bye to me, and gestures for Jonathan to join her at her car. He starts to walk away from me, then turns back and meets my curious eyes. "I have to admit that I'm glad Ryan's gone, but I think he must have been good for you. You're different from when I met you a month ago. And … " He pauses while I take that in.

"And?"

"Thank you for saying yes."

"Sure," I say, getting into my car with a smile. "I'm looking forward to it."

As I rev up my car and turn on the heater, I realize that I'm looking forward to experiencing the Halloween Scavenger Hunt with Jonathan. I didn't say yes because Ryan is gone and I was feeling lonely. I said yes because I want to spend more time with Jonathan. And also, because it sounds like fun. So much fun.

I sit still, pondering what Jonathan just said—about me being different from when he met me last month, about how Ryan must have been good for me. I think back on what my life was like when I met Ryan, and how I was drawn to him because he reminded me of someone. There was something in him that I recognized.

Jonathan was right—these changes in me *are* because of Ryan. What I recognized in Ryan was *myself.* The liveliness, the reaching out to others with lightheartedness and eager good humor. That ability to make people feel that zest for life. The ability to feel joy. To say *yes*.

Early on in my relationship with Marc, I once heard him describing me to Vivian during a phone call. "She has a certain joie de vivre," he said. "She finds joy in living. That's what I love most about her."

*Joie de vivre.*

No wonder Ryan seemed so familiar! I was wrong when I told him I'd never met anyone like him before … because I'd already met *myself.* Although, along the way, I had lost her to two years of obstinate, desperate grief.

What a relief, what a joy, to connect with her—with myself—again.

As I drive home and settle into bed with a sleepy Jezebel draped across my feet, I whisper a quick prayer of gratitude for Ryan. Perhaps we were "meant to be" after all, just in a different way than what those words usually mean.

# Chapter 16

*"So," Camille says,* beaming at me through the laptop screen. "You've had a quite a month, haven't you?"

"I guess I have," I reply, trying to hide a smile but failing. We've been talking for a while. Rather, I've been talking and she's been listening—her fingers forming a steeple, her kind eyes focused on me. I'm at my kitchen table; Camille is in her Brighton office, sitting in her stylish office chair. I can see bare tree branches and a vivid blue October sky through the window behind her. She's holding a delicate floral teacup in her hands.

"I'm proud of you for going to see Vivian and telling her about the baby … about Finn. I hoped you would do that when you were ready."

"Carlos said the exact same thing!"

"How is he doing?"

"Great, as always. He and Jasper … I'm so happy for them both."

"And how has it been without Ryan?"

I pause now, thinking back over the last few weeks. "It was strange at first. I mean, I missed him. A lot." Jezebel jumps onto the kitchen table and pushes at the screen with an inky black paw.

Camille laughs. "Hello, Jezebel! Are you keeping your mama company?"

I pull Jez onto my lap. "She's great company and I'll be forever grateful to you for challenging me to take her in." Jez purrs loudly and rubs her head against my chin.

"Don't change the subject. I was asking about Ryan. Have you heard from him?"

"We've texted a few times. He's had several callbacks from his latest audition, so things are looking good. He might come to opening night of *Our Town*, but I've tried to prepare the kids for the fact that he might not show. He's kind of a celebrity around here, and they're excited about seeing him again."

"And you?"

"I'm not sure. I mean, he was a big help with the play after Jonathan stopped him from changing the set pieces to modern day New York City."

"Oh my!"

"I wouldn't mind seeing him again, but I know our time together was a once-in-a-lifetime thing that can't be repeated."

"Would you like it to be repeated?"

Jezebel jumps from my lap, lands lightly on the floor, and walks daintily to her water bowl. "Not at all. You know, I realized something the other day. I was drawn to Ryan from the beginning because there was something so familiar about him, but I couldn't put my finger on what it was. Now that he's gone, I realize that he reminded me of myself. Me. Before Marc died."

"Interesting. I didn't know you before your loss, but even now, through the computer screen, you do seem different."

"I do?"

"Yes. Your eyes are brighter, your posture is straighter. I sense a whole different energy about you. It's like … " Camille swivels in her chair and looks out the window for a while, before turning back to the screen. "It's like you've shed the heaviness of your grief. It seems to not be weighing you down anymore."

I lean forward, palms resting on the table. "That's it exactly! I mean, I'm still carrying the loss, but it feels like I've somehow grown a space inside of me that's big enough to hold it, so it doesn't hurt like it used to. Someone at the TNA group talked about that at my first meeting, and it makes sense to me now."

"It sounds like you've learned a lot about yourself in the short time that you've been in Seahaven."

"I have," I murmur.

"Do you think you need some closure with Ryan?"

"What do you mean?"

"What do you think I mean?"

Oh boy, there she goes again. My therapist with the gazillion fascinating questions. I shift uneasily in my seat. "I guess you mean that I should talk with Ryan person-to-person. Instead of texting. To make sure he's clear that this is an ending."

Camille sits on the edge of her chair and puts her face closer to the camera until her nose is almost touching the screen. "What do you think about that?"

"I think it's a good idea, but … "

"Go on."

"For one thing, I've never had to have this kind of conversation with a guy before. It feels like I'm breaking up with him, but we never talked about what our relationship was and wasn't, so it's not really breaking up. Is it?"

"All of that, my dear, is exactly why you should have the conversation with him now. From what you told me, it sounds like your relationship was a temporary thing and that both of you had that understanding. Even if it was unspoken."

"I always had that understanding, and I assumed that he did too." I pause, drumming my fingers on my laptop as I watch Jezebel methodically chase a catnip mouse around the kitchen floor. "Which, I suppose, is exactly why I need to talk with him now. I've been assuming something that might not be true." I sigh and offer Camille a playful salute. "This is why I pay you the big bucks. You always know what I need."

Camille chuckles. "I don't know about that, Elena. Just remember, going forward, your job is to continue to stay in touch with what *you* need."

We're silent for a few long moments as I let this sink in. I am imagining a life where I don't depend on Camille for pointing out what I need to feel, think, or do. It feels strange, but right.

Our conversation continues as I tell her how the talk of Tess and Luca's wedding reminded me of my own special day, and how that memory made me smile for the first time since Marc died. The edges of those memories are no longer sharp and painful, but smoother and more even, like the several pieces of colorful sea glass that rest on the table beside me. My collection is beginning to grow.

"Yes, the memories will fade but they won't go away completely. It sounds like you're already looking at those memories of Marc through different eyes than when you first came to me."

She's right. That's exactly what is happening. I am glad to have the memories, glad to know that they will always be with me, glad that they have softened with time and no longer cause pain. I never thought this day would come … but here it is.

When our time is up, instead of scheduling our next appointment, Camille asks if we need to meet again. I look at her in wonder. "Do you honestly think I'm ready to stop seeing you?"

"It's entirely up to you."

"But do you think I can … handle life on my own now?"

"Do *you* think you're ready to let me go? And *are* you truly on your own? Those are the only two questions to consider right now."

I look down at Jezebel who is taking her own sweet time as she repeatedly licks a paw and washes her face. "I think I might be *almost* ready," I say with a tentative smile. "But could I have one more session?"

Camille nods and pulls out her appointment book. "Of course. We'll talk more then. I look forward to it."

As soon as I wave good-bye to Camille and close my laptop, I grab my phone and head to the rocking chair. Settling in, I close my eyes for a minute and think of my mother. Her name was Clarita Fuentes and this was her favorite chair. Someday, if I have a daughter, I would like to name her Clarita, or maybe Claire. My memories of Mama are scented with her Alegria perfume and gilded with the familiar, welcome sight of her at our kitchen table. I can almost feel her arms around me and distinctly remember the taste of her mouthwatering food.

Camille was right; these memories of my mother were painful at first, but they have softened over the years.

I think of her now and smile as I call Ryan on Facetime. Mama always had a gentle way of letting me down, telling me no, handling my disappointment. May I handle this conversation as gently as she would have.

"Hey, Elena!" Ryan's face bursts through the screen and the sight of him makes me smile. "I'm so glad you called. How's it goin'?" He's holding his phone a few feet away from his face as he walks down a busy street in New York City. There are people everywhere; the noise of cars and trucks and strangers makes for some annoying yet interesting background static.

"I'm doing great. You?"

"Awesome. I was just at my agent's office where I signed a one-year contract to star in *You're So Fine* on Broadway! It's a new work, written and directed by Lin-Manuel Miranda! Can you believe it?" I can hear the palpable excitement in his voice. It's the middle of the afternoon but even if it was the darkest night, his smile would light up the cyberspace between us.

"You bet I believe it! Ryan, that's amazing. I'm so happy for you!"

"I'm almost home." He turns a corner and enters a brick building. "Tell me what's going on in Seahaven."

"The kids are doing great with the play, as you already know. Also, there's something happening next weekend called The Great Big Seahaven Halloween Scavenger Hunt."

"Whoa, that sounds fun," he replies, zipping up a flight of stairs and unlocking his apartment door.

"I think it will be," I say carefully, not sure if I should mention that I'm going with Jonathan. But then I think, why not? "I'm going to do the scavenger hunt with Jonathan … Mr. MacKenna."

Ryan drops his denim knapsack on the floor and plops onto a threadbare sofa. "Oh yeah, Mr. Mac. I really like him."

"Me too. Listen, do you have a few minutes to talk?"

"Sure!" He drapes his legs over the side of the sofa and runs a hand through his curly blonde hair which looks longer than I remember. "What's up?"

I clear my throat. How to begin? "First of all, I think it's wonderful that your dream of starring on Broadway is coming true. I'm so happy for you."

He grins and, even though we are miles apart, speaking through technology instead of face to face, his smile touches my heart.

"And I want to tell you that I'm glad our paths crossed when they did. Fate or destiny or synchronicity … whatever you want to call it … I'm glad that I met you."

Ryan holds the phone closer to his face. "I'm glad I met you too, Elena. Really glad."

I rock gently in Mama's chair. "Remember how I used to say that you reminded me of someone?"

He nods, and I see in his eyes that he is listening with his heart.

"I finally figured out that you reminded me of myself, before Marc died. I used to be like you—outgoing, fun, vivacious. See, I had lost that part of myself and I didn't even know it until you came along. So I want to say thank you. Thank you for being you and for inviting me into your life the way you did."

He sits up now and rests his elbows on his knees. "It was a pleasure, and you should know that you let me into *your* life too."

"Okay, it was a two-way street," I say, feeling happy at his response. It's true. Unexpected as it was, I did open up and let him in. "Anyway, I also want to say that I think our relationship has run its course. I mean, we never defined our relationship. I was always aware that we were a temporary thing and I hope that you—"

I see Ryan's hand, palm facing out like a stop sign. "Elena, you were … you are like a breath of fresh air to me, and I also always knew that we weren't meant to be for the long haul. I'm glad to hear that you knew it too. I don't want you to think that I was casual about our time together or that it was just for fun." He shakes his head before continuing. "I'm glad I met you too."

"That's good to hear," I say, laughing with relief. "I was afraid you were expecting me to drive down to New York every weekend or something."

"Maybe just once?" he says with a smile. "To see me on Broadway? Maybe you and Mr. Mac … I mean, maybe you and Jonathan could come together?"

"Okay, you talked me into it. I'll see what he thinks."

"And hey, it's true that we weren't meant to be a couple, but do you think it's possible that we're meant to be friends?"

"Yes, Ryan, that's exactly what I think."

He reaches into his jeans pocket and pulls out the milky white piece of sea glass that I gave him the day we watched the Seahaven sunrise, a day that seems so long ago now. "I still have this," he says. "It stays in my pocket as a reminder."

"Of me?"

"Definitely you, as well as the fact that when I experience a loss as deep as yours, I'll be able to survive it. Like you did."

We continue to talk for a while, shifting easily into the new definition of our relationship. I feel relieved and can breathe more easily now. It's doing me good to take charge of my life again, to pay attention to what I need.

A few days later, Tess invites me to walk with her to Coastal Soul, Kit's shop downtown. "I need to start thinking about Halloween and the Scavenger Hunt," she says as we head down Bright Blessing Way.

I've been inside all morning going over my notes for *Our Town*, and the fresh air feels good on my face. Although the sky is a brilliant blue and the sun shines overhead, the wind from the ocean is brisk and we're both wearing our winter coats.

"Do you know what you're going to wear?" Tess asks.

"Wear?" I'm enjoying the sound of the fallen leaves crunching under my feet as we walk to town. It's not that far, thank goodness.

"If you're going to the Scavenger Hunt, you'll need to wear a costume. Eva and I are thinking of going as Lorelai and Rory. You know, from *Gilmore Girls*?"

I laugh. "Of course. I love that show. In fact, I binge-watched it a few times during my three-month sabbatical after Marc died. It made me laugh when I didn't think I would ever laugh again. It was comforting somehow. Hey, you and Eva are also Gilmore girls! Those should be easy costumes to put together. What about Luca? Is he going to dress as Luke?"

"I'm trying to talk him into it. He doesn't get the thing about the show."

"What about his son? Teo could go as Dean or Jess or Logan!"

It's Tess's turn to laugh now. "I'd probably have to talk him into that. If I know Eva, she'd dress him up as Rory's first boyfriend, Dean, but if I know Teo, he's going to want to go as Spider Man or whoever the superhero of the day is right now. What about you?"

We cross Maine Street and turn left. Two more blocks to Coastal Soul. "I haven't thought about it. The last time I put on a costume, Marc and I went as Mr. Darcy and Elizabeth Bennett." I smile. Another memory that finally feels smooth in my mind. "It was a Halloween party at his office."

"That sounds like fun," Tess agrees. "Eva and I haven't ever dressed up together, so this will be a first."

We quickly climb the three concrete steps—each painted with a vivid array of rainbow colors—that lead us into Kit's shop. A quartet of silvery chimes greet us sweetly as we open the turquoise door. There are several people already inside, perusing the copious shelves and displays. I pause at the doorway and breathe in. It smells divine, like jasmine and roses, but there's something more earthy underneath it all. Incense maybe?

"I'm heading back to the books section," Tess says, leaving me to wander around the front of the store. There's so much here to discover—unusual jewelry, handmade bookmarks, crystal statues, pretty soaps. It's a bit overwhelming.

That's when I see it.

I stop abruptly in front of a framed watercolor painting of the ocean. The water is vibrant in deep teals and turquoise, the sand a soft ivory that seems to sparkle. The sky above the water is pale blue, stroked with lavender and rose, perhaps the beginning of a sunrise or the end of a sunset. The imagery is stunning, but what has stopped me in my tracks are the dark blue scripted words that lift into the sky—

*There was another life that I might have had,*
*but I am having this one.*
~ **Kazuo Ishiguro**

"It's beautiful, isn't it?" Kit is standing beside me, her arm touching mine. She is gazing at it with the same intensity as my own.

"Yes." That's about all I can say before I'm reaching for it, holding the plain oak frame in my trembling hands, clasping it to my chest. It's almost too much to process. Fifteen words, all of which I've heard before, but never strung together quite like this. Yes, there was another life I might have had—a long life where I grew old with Marc and our children, maybe even a few grandchildren. I might have had that life. But that life was interrupted. A senseless accident on a cold November afternoon. No one's fault. Bad timing. Whatever. And now … now, I'm not having *that* life. I'm living a different life. Different from the one I expected, different from the one I had wanted.

I feel my eyes glisten with tears but they are not tears of sadness. They are tears of recognition and wonder. This is my life now. *This* one. Here in Seahaven. With Marc in my heart instead of in my arms.

A simple but provocative awareness floods my heart—I am meant to *live* this life, not merely exist in it. I'm meant to have *this* life now. It is mine to own, to revel in, to enjoy. This realization makes my heart open a little wider to any possibilities that might be ahead of me.

"I can see that this one resonates with you, dear." Kit pats my shoulder gently; her empathy seeps through my winter coat, down to my soul. "Believe me, I understand. Come, I'll wrap it up for you. We'll give you the family discount."

# Chapter 17

## KIT GILMORE

*Kit gazed at* the watercolor painting before laying it down onto a large section of eco-friendly paper wrap.

*There was another life*
*that I might have had*
*but I am having this one.*

She was familiar with this Japanese-British author, Kazuo Ishiguro, and had read a few of his novels. The colors of the painting that accompany the stirring quotation reminded her of the thousands of Seahaven sunrises she'd experienced since that cold February morning—six weeks after Ollie's death—in Lillian's Jeep. Sunrises not only in coastal Maine, but all over the world—some bold, some pale; some memorable, some easily forgotten; some clouded over, some brilliant and breathtaking.

*Just like the days of one's life*, she mused.

Her fingers traced the words slowly and the soft lighting of Coastal Soul faded along with the peaceful music from the store's speakers and the sound of customers chatting in the background.

Yes, there was another life that Kit might have had. She might have graduated from UMO with a degree in elementary education, married Ollie right away, taught kindergarten for a few years, then gotten pregnant and raised a family with him. That had been the plan, and it had been a great plan. The best plan ever. She smiled as she studied the framed sunrise, remembering the love that she and Ollie had shared. A once-in-a-lifetime, kindred love—that's what they had called it.

But Life had intervened. Kit had been left behind ... to live another life. Quite *different* from the life she might have had. Not *better,* yet—surprisingly enough, when viewed from today—not *worse* either.

As she carefully pulled the edges of the brown paper over the sides of the painting and secured them with tape for Elena, she thought back on how her life had unfolded after that unexpected wake-up call at Sunrise Beach with Ollie's mom.

Some days she slept later than others, but slowly and surely, she had gotten out of bed each day at the Mattheson house. Lillian and Olivia were there for her in ways that her own family was unable to be.

The next summer, after several months of learning to make space inside her heart for her sorrow, she got a job waitressing in York at the Stage Neck Inn—an elegant, upscale restaurant with magnificent ocean views. When September came, she decided to keep working there because the money was good and she couldn't imagine herself sitting in a classroom, particularly not on the campus that was so flooded with memories of Ollie. She made friends with another waitress, Violet, and they rented an apartment together on Main Street in Seahaven over the Sea Star Candy Shop. Together, they drove down the coast to Portsmouth, New Hampshire every Sunday and volunteered at the Big Brother Big

Sisters organization. It had felt so good to continue sharing Ollie's light with the world in this way.

One Friday night the following summer, a handsome blond man in his thirties and his attractive, equally-blond wife were dining in Kit's section at the restaurant. They were on vacation from New York City and were inquisitive about the area. She enjoyed sharing information with them about where to go and what to see on the Maine coast.

As the couple was getting ready to leave, the blond man handed Kit his card. "I'm an agent in New York. Give me a call if you're interested in a career that would take you out of here." His words were sincere, and Kit's hand trembled a bit as she took his card. *Marshall Sorenson.* The words were etched in gold on a background of satiny navy, along with his phone number, address, and the astonishing words *Talent Agent.*

Noticing Kit's skeptical expression, his wife smiled and said, "Don't worry, he's legit. I can vouch for him. He has an eye for the very best."

"Of course, I do. I married you, didn't I?" Marshall kissed his wife on the cheek. "This is Cassie, and she's right—I do have a good eye."

Kit looked around to see if any of the diners in her section needed anything before continuing this bewildering conversation. "But why would you … I mean, I'm no good at singing and I've never even acted before." She held the card out as if to give it back.

"I'd like to send you to a few modeling agencies," Marshall replied. "You've got it all—face, hair, and eyes. Your entire physical appearance is classically beautiful."

"Modeling jobs?" Kit repeated. Sure, Ollie had told her she was beautiful—many, many times—and when she looked in the mirror, she usually liked what she saw. But she couldn't picture herself on the cover of a magazine or on a fashion runway. Her mother had called beauty magazines "a waste of time," and preached about the dangers of vanity whenever Kit tried a new hairstyle or bought a new outfit.

"Take some time to think about it, then give me a call," Marshall said with a kind smile. "What have you got to lose?"

Marshall had been right—she didn't have anything to lose. Ollie was gone. Her mother wanted nothing to do with her unless she went back to college. Frank had already married and had started his own independent insurance business in Connecticut. She still stayed in touch with her dad; they had lunch together every Monday in York.

Kit hadn't called Marshall right away. She couldn't imagine living anywhere but Maine, close to her treasured memories of Ollie. But Marshall and Cassie came back to the restaurant a few times that month and she found them both charming and sophisticated, yet down-to-earth and authentic.

Kit had coffee with Marshall a few times before her shift at the restaurant. He entertained her with stories about life in New York, and the possibilities inherent in her potential new career. She had been considering going back to college in January for the winter semester, but the more she thought about it, the more she discovered her desire for teaching had faded. Teaching was an old dream, a dream that was meant for her and Ollie. Together.

When she shared this with Marshall, he encouraged her to follow her heart, to take a chance, to let the more rational voices in her mind fade away. Her heart was still longing for Ollie, but she was resigned now to the fact that her heart was not going to get what her heart wanted. Perhaps her heart could have something else instead. This was a new idea, one that startled her into dismissing the prevailing thought that she should go back to school.

Increasingly intrigued by the idea of a different kind of life, Kit invited Marshall and Cassie to a cookout at Lillian's one evening that summer, and with Lillian and Olivia's blessing, she finally agreed to one—just one—audition.

No one was more surprised than Kit (and maybe Jane) when her modeling career took off almost from the minute she set foot in New York City. Looking back on it all now, she realized how young she had been, but at the time it had all been very exciting. Moving forward with her life in such a shocking way—traveling to unfamiliar, exotic locations like Paris, Barcelona, Milan, and London—was tremendously helpful as she continued to leave her memories in the past. It had been two years since Ollie had died. She was ready to let go of her grief, but she would never let go of Ollie. He traveled with her in her heart, in the ring that she still wore on her left hand, and in the framed photo that was always tucked into the side pocket of her carry-on bag. Ollie with the curly brown hair and the smiling hazel eyes that had always looked into hers with such blessing and love.

She started out modeling clothing, and after a few years found herself specialized in jobs that focused on her hair and face. She was making better-than-good money; it had never crossed her mind that a person could earn so much while standing still and being photographed. Not that it was always easy. Sometimes the hours were grueling, the lights harsh, and the photographers demanding.

But not always. She made friends with some of the women and men who appeared on the same photo shoots, enjoyed several lovers over the years, and did her fair share of partying and drinking in her twenties and early thirties. Parties on yachts, private jets to wherever she needed to go. She called it an "adventurous lifestyle," although she often wondered what Ollie would think of the choices she was making. She started smoking, a habit that she never thought she would acquire, but she never tried cocaine or any of the multi-colored pills that made the rounds at some of the parties she was invited to.

She was becoming well-known in professional circles—and to the public—as simply "Katharine," which should have made her mother happy, but Jane did not want anything to do with a daughter who had no college education, a daughter whose suddenly-recognizable face was splashed across magazines and made prominent on billboards throughout all the major cities in America and beyond. Kit had long ago accepted that her mother and she were on two entirely different wavelengths, so she took solace in the love and encouragement from Lillian, Olivia, Violet, the Sorensons, and her father.

Whenever she had a break in her schedule, she flew directly back to Seahaven and stayed in the Mattheson guest room—rising early most mornings for sunrise walks with Lillian, shopping trips to Freeport, and catch-up lunches with Olivia and Violet. Seahaven was her home base. She got together with her dad now and then, but it was those times with her friends and Lillian that grounded her.

Kit wore Ollie's engagement ring until her thirtieth birthday, which she celebrated with Lillian and Olivia in Seahaven, in between modeling jobs. On that day—February 2, 1989—she walked Sunrise Beach alone and had a long conversation with Ollie in her mind.

*I will always love you, and the fact that I am taking off your ring—our ring—doesn't mean anything except that I want to keep it somewhere safe. I don't need a ring on my finger to remind me of our time together.*

When she got home, she kissed the ring, held it tightly in her hand for a few minutes, then returned it to the blue velvet box that Ollie had opened when he asked her to marry him. She gave it to Lillian for safe-keeping and now it rested in the top dresser drawer of her cottage bedroom, directly under the small altar where she kept her favorite photo of Ollie and a few memories of their relationship.

As time went on, she was recognized more and more due to her ads for hair styling products and salons. At the beginning, her light brown hair was thick and full, streaked with golden highlights. A hairdresser's dream. In her mid-forties, that hair skipped right past gray and softened into an alluring shade of silver. Also a hairdresser's dream. At that time, she was still in demand for ads featuring hair care products, because not only was her hair lustrous and silver, it was still long and thick.

Once she began accumulating wealth, Marshall introduced her to her current business manager, Andrea Sweeter. Andrea helped Kit carry Ollie's light to the world in a much bigger way. Kit supported the Big Brothers Big Sisters Association with annual donations that were larger than the cost of most peoples' houses. These gifts were given in the name of Oliver Sean Mattheson—her way of making sure that his memory would never be forgotten. Kit was also an active media spokeswoman for that organization, and on the Board of Directors of the International Literary Association.

About ten years ago she had let go of the modeling contracts and settled in Seahaven. She bought the old Victorian on Bright Blessing Way, renovated it into four spacious apartments, painted it a comforting buttery yellow, and built herself the cozy matching yellow cottage at the edge of the property. Her mother died first, then Carson shortly after. Each death was difficult for Kit in its own way. She had made peace with the fact that she would never be close to her mother, but that didn't stop her from grieving that particular loss. As for Carson, Kit still keenly missed his comforting presence and ability to offer unconditional love, along with his wacky sense of humor.

She took out the engagement ring from time to time to relive her favorite Ollie memories, but never again put it on her finger. As she watched Tess and Luca's relationship blossom and turn into plans for a wedding, Kit thought she might ask Tess if she wanted to wear it on her wedding day as the traditional "something borrowed." Yes, that was a good plan, and she would wait for the exact right moment to mention it to her beloved niece.

"Kit? Is the picture wrapped up yet? Tess is waiting for me. She's ready to leave." Elena's voice interrupted Kit's reverie, bringing her back to Coastal Soul, the large table cluttered with various sizes of scissors, colorful rolls of paper, and brown packing wrap. A gentle Carrie Newcomer song drifted through the shop's speaker system.

"Yes, yes, it's almost done." She folded the top and bottom of the wrapping paper into the center of the package and applied more tape, then tucked it into a lavender bag with white handles. "Here you go, dear. Take it to the front and Samantha will ring it up for you. Remind her about the family discount."

"I will, thank you." Elena turned to leave, then hesitated. "Are you sure that you should be back here, working so soon after your heart event?"

Kit brought both hands to her flushed face and smoothed her famous hair behind her ears. "Of course! I'm perfectly fine. Why would you say that?

"You looked like you were a million miles away just now, that's all."

"A million miles away in thought. I was thinking about the life I might have had—with Ollie—and measuring it against the life I have now."

"And?" Expectant curiosity wove its way through Elena's question.

Kit paused, looked around the store, then back at her young friend. "It's my life, exactly as it's supposed to be right now. It's the life I created, even when I thought nothing would ever matter again." She paused. "And so it will be for you."

Leaning across the wrapping table to give Kit a quick hug, Elena blinked back tears. She was beginning to believe that it was true.

# Chapter 18

## ELENA

*The Great Big* Seahaven Halloween Scavenger Hunt on Saturday is much bigger and wilder than I imagined. Hundreds of people—young, old, and everything in between—are gathered on the Seahaven Common downtown. It's mid-afternoon and there's a brisk breeze blowing off the ocean.

"I'm seeing a whole other side of you," I say, peering at Jonathan who is wearing a pirate costume, complete with tri-corner black hat, matching boots, and an incredibly sexy eye patch. This pirate is sporting nerdy eyeglasses over the patch, but still.

Wait. Did I just say *sexy*? Hmmm …

This feels like another side of him not just because of his costume (I imagined he would dress up as Benjamin Franklin or some other historical figure) but because his father has just announced the R&R's—Rules and Regulations—over a rather wonky sound system and Jonathan is impatiently shuffling his feet as he opens the app on his tablet that has the list of items we're supposed to find. He's like a racehorse at the starting line, although there's no clear step off point here. We are a magnificent mass of unorganized people, most of us in costume. I can feel the excitement of the crowd lifting from chattering voices and excited faces, up and up through the stately pine trees and bare elms that surround the Common, and into the cloudy afternoon sky.

Jonathan smiles and nudges my elbow, glancing up for two seconds from his tablet where he's been intensely scanning the list. "I see another side of you, too."

I wonder what other side of me Jonathan sees. He might be referring to the *Where's Waldo* outfit that I bought at the BackStage Shop in Brunswick last week when I picked up the costumes for *Our Town.* It's simple enough—a red and white striped long-sleeved sweater and my oldest pair of jeans—but I've tucked my hair into the matching striped knit cap and donned a pair of fake round spectacles. In addition, I put a heavy white turtleneck under the shirt. I know Waldo doesn't wear a turtleneck, but I have a feeling this is going to be a chilly evening. I even have the rounded brown cane, and I've painted some freckles on my face. It's true, Waldo doesn't have freckles, but I thought it would be fun. I'm grateful I chose this costume because it's much warmer than what some people are wearing! On the other side of the crowd, I spy Kit and Marshall who are dressed as Bonnie and Clyde. They're holding hands and laughing at something that Bea Lively—dressed in an outrageous clown costume—is saying.

"How does this work and what do we have to find exactly?" I'm trying to catch a glimpse of his tablet but he's scrutinizing it too carefully.

"We're all waiting for my dad to give the signal and we'll be on our way." He looks up at the platform in the center of the Common where his father stands with three other townspeople who apparently are on the Steering Committee. "The thing is, we need to have a strategy. We can't just run off willy-nilly."

I laugh out loud, then clap a hand over my mouth. "Willy-nilly? I haven't heard that phrase in a long time."

Jonathan frowns and scrolls through the list again.

"*Mr. Mac,* are you going to enlighten me with your strategy so I can perhaps … help?"

"What?" He looks at me but I can tell he's still seeing—or maybe memorizing—the list.

"We're a team, right? Isn't the whole point to have fun with the team?"

His shoulders finally relax and he looks at me again; I can tell he's actually seeing me this time. "Yes, we are a team, and we're going to be a good one. The best. Because we're going to win this thing!" He makes a fist and jams his elbow down against his waist as if we've already won.

I tap my Waldo cane on the ground, then poke his foot gently with it. "Have you won this thing before?"

"No, never." He shakes his head sadly. I look for signs of theatrics, but he is seriously disappointed. He clearly wants to win this time, so I'm going to try my best to make today the first time he does. The first time *we* do. Did I just say *first*? Did I just say *we*? Do I anticipate that we might be doing this again next year … and the year after that? I put my hand on his shoulder and am about to encourage him, but we're interrupted by a ghastly, distorted horn blast from the center platform. It sounds like a clumsy bugle player blurting out several sour notes in quick succession.

Suddenly, the crowd is in motion, shouting and laughing, scurrying off to who-knows-where to find whatever is on this list. But Jonathan stands still—a tall, calm presence in the midst of chaos. I find myself admiring that about him when he grabs my hand (why didn't I think to bring mittens?) and guides me to one of the benches near the sidewalk on the west side of the Common. We sit and he angles his body toward me. "First, we're going to look at the list together. Here." He scoots a little closer to me so I can see the tablet. Our heads are bent and my knit cap is touching the side of his face. I know I'm supposed to be looking at the tablet, but I'm distracted by his proximity—the way his shoulder feels against mine. He smells like wisps of wood smoke and salty apples. I could get used to this scent.

"Elena?" He snaps his fingers as if to wake me up. "There are three categories of items on the list." He taps an impatient finger on his tablet. I force myself to pay attention.

The categories are *Things to Pick Up*, *Facts to Discover,* and *Photos/Videos to Upload.* There are six things on each list. I didn't think there would be so many, but I'm game for anything now. It's cold out here and we need to get moving. If not to find everything, at least to warm up. "Okay, I get it. Now, what's our strategy?"

"The rule is that we stick together. No separating. I tried to change that when I was on the Scavenger Hunt Committee, because more can be accomplished when we divide up the list ... " He shrugs. "But I was outvoted. Evidently, it's all about *teamwork.* Why don't I take all the photos and videos? You write down all the facts, and we can each carry some of the things to bring."

"I don't have a pen or paper." I look around frantically. There are still a few people hanging around the Common. It's time to get going if he seriously wants to win.

"No worries," he replies cheerfully, standing up and reaching into one of his pirate pockets. I didn't know that pirates actually had pockets, but Jonathan has apparently thought of everything. He hands me a small notebook with a magnetic pen attached to the binding. "Here you go, Waldo!"

I take the notebook as he reaches into another pocket and hands me a cloth bag, about the size of a composition book. "Wow, you came prepared!"

He chuckles and looks back at the list with a proud smile. "I've been doing this for many years."

"Tell me the truth. Since your father is in charge, aren't you able to get advance notice of what's on the list?"

"Shiver me timbers, lass!" he exclaims in a distinct pirate-like accent as he slaps one hand over his heart. "That would be cheating and MacKennas do not cheat."

I try to hide my grin. "So … we have to stay together, and everything gets turned in by eight o'clock tonight?"

"That's right. We're going to save the mask-making project at the Community Center 'til around seven o'clock. That way we'll already be there at eight when it's time to turn everything in. And while we're creating the mask, we can write and record our little Halloween song to the tune of *Yankee Doodle.* That's the last thing on our list. Get it all done in one fell swoop, timely and efficient. Okay, Waldo … are you ready?"

"I'm ready!" I clap my hands in what might be called actual excitement. "What's first on the list?"

Jonathan's plan, I must admit, is quite clever. As we walk across the Common, brown and gold leaves crunching under our feet, he informs me that he's studied all three of the lists and grouped the items together by location.

The first place we head is half a mile down the main road to get a photo of the Welcome to Seahaven town sign. Funny, I've driven by it several times since moving here, but I never noticed the slogan before: *A Harbor of Safety for All Who Pass Through.* I slowly read the sign out loud, as Jonathan hurriedly takes the picture and begins to walk away.

"Elena? Let's go!" He turns impatiently and lifts his hands as if to ask me what the heck I'm doing still standing at the sign.

There's a lump in my throat and I swallow hard. "I'm moved by the Seahaven slogan, that's all," I finally say.

His face rearranges itself from annoyance to the kindness that I'm accustomed to seeing there. "It's a good one," he agrees as he holds my gaze and waits for me to take the first step away. "We could head out that way … " He points down the side street that leads to Chloe's by the Sea. "… because the list of photos includes one of Chloe."

"Great restaurant."

"It is. However, this was on the list last year too, but no one has ever been able to get a picture of her. I don't know why she's on the list again this time."

"That's strange. Isn't she the head chef and doesn't she own the restaurant? I was with Kit's family when her boyfriend guessed the secret ingredient, but she didn't come out and shake his hand. We were surprised that the head chef didn't want to meet him."

"It's all quite mysterious." Jonathan shakes his head. "Mysterious and very, very weird. No one even knows where she lives, and she's not listed in the town directory. I say we don't even try to get the photo. Let's head down Sugar Shores Road instead to see if someone has a gravestone decoration on their lawn. We need a photo of that next."

Luck is with us because halfway down this little side street that runs parallel to Bright Blessing Way, there's an intentionally spooky display of a blow-up haunted house with several plastic gravestones in front of it. The stones are engraved with silly epitaphs like *Guy O'Tine: Worked Hard to Get Ahead*; *Fiona Fibber: I Told You I Was Sick*; and *Here Lies Riggor Mortis: He Died a Little Stiff.*

Jonathan and I double over with laughter, especially at the last one.

He takes the photo and as we begin to move on, I find myself wondering about Marc's tombstone. At his funeral, Vivian told me that she would take care of it, and even though she was kind enough to ask me what I wanted engraved on it, I was in so much shock that I had no idea what it ought to say. I hate to admit this, but I left it all up to her. I did go to the cemetery a few times after the funeral, but the stone wasn't in place yet. After I lost Finn, I was so flattened with grief that I couldn't bring myself to go back there. Besides, I knew even then that I didn't need to go to Marc's grave in order to talk to him. I wonder what Vivian decided to put on Marc's memorial stone.

"Hey, this would be a good place to make the five-second video of us singing 'Monster Mash'," Jonathan says excitedly, turning back to the haunted house display.

This startles me, but I discover that I'm able to let go of my murky memories and join Jonathan in a horrendous rendition of the chorus. Several other scavenger hunters and trick-or-treaters are laughing with us and cheering us on.

As we continue around town, I make note of the Facts to Discover in the little notebook with my partially frozen fingers:

Combined ages of Framuel—Fred and Samuel—from Simply Sweets: 136
Date Seahaven was founded and by whom: 1654, Reginald Quimby and Elias Stark
Name of new Halloween sandwich at Sunnyside Up: Monster Meatball Sub
Number of pumpkins in window at Coastal Soul: 14
Celtic holiday that Halloween is derived from: Samhain
Costumes the dentists are wearing at Pearly Whites: toothbrushes (1 pink, 1 green)

While we're at the Pearly Whites Dental Office, I grab a sugar free lollipop and add it to my treasure bag next to the acorn we picked up before we left the Common. As we trek around town, several of our students stop and say hello. Most of them are giggling at "Mr. Mac's" costume, but they admire mine too.

We pause outside of Bright Side Animal Clinic, looking for *something hidden in one of the window boxes.* This clue is not so easy because the two big window boxes on the parking lot side of the building are filled with dirt. I am using my cane to poke around in the dirt of one box while Jonathan is using his hands in the other, when Dr. Brightman exits the building. "Hey there!" he calls, followed by my brother along with Carolina who I met when I brought Jezebel in for her check-up.

"Hi Dr. Brightman! Carlos and Carolina, this is Jonathan MacKenna."

"Sure, we know Jonathan," Dr. Brightman says, striding over to us and attempting to shake Jonathan's dirty hand. He reconsiders and claps him on the shoulder instead. "Good to see you again. How is Misty doing these days?"

"Misty?" I interject.

"I have a cocker spaniel," he whispers to me, then faces the others. "She's doing great, Doc, but we're kind of in a hurry here. We're on the scavenger hunt and we're trying to find something hidden in one of your window boxes but there doesn't seem to be anything here." I notice Carolina and Carlos exchange amused glances.

"Not sure what to tell you," Dr. Brightman says, backing away from us with a mischievous smile. He looks to be fifty-something, with sparse brown hair combed back from his ordinary face. His eyes are a pleasant shade of grayish blue with laugh lines spanning out from them. Jezebel hadn't squirmed away when he examined her. In fact, she had downright purred as soon as he started stroking her black fur. I liked him immediately.

"Hey, why aren't you guys doing the scavenger hunt?" I call as they head to their cars. "Where are your costumes?"

Carolina pushes her flaming red, curly hair over her shoulder as she opens the car door. "It's too late to participate in the hunt, but you'll see me as Bette Midler from *Hocus Pocus* at the Halloween Party later.

"Party?"

"Yes, it's at eight o'clock, after everyone turns in their findings." Jonathan stage whispers to me from the corner of his mouth. "Didn't you hear what my father said when he was giving out the R&Rs?"

Apparently not. I begin to reply but then I notice Carlos beckoning us. I start to move toward him, but he puts a finger to his lips. With his other hand, he holds up each finger, one at a time, then waves them at us as he wiggles his eyebrows and smirks knowingly.

"What the—"

"I've got it!" Jonathan exclaims. There are five window boxes, not just two! We've got to find the other three."

I blow a quick kiss of gratitude to Carlos as he backs out of the parking lot with a jaunty wave.

Jonathan and I cautiously look around to make sure no other scavenger hunters are following us as we make our way around the building. Sure enough, there are two more planters on the side, and one in the back. Bingo! The one in the back has a large vinyl envelope tucked into the dirt. I open it up and take out a slip of paper printed with a funny Halloween limerick about dogs and cats, written by Dr. Brightman himself. Jezebel's new vet is proving to be a man of many talents.

"This is a good find," Jonathan says happily as we head to the beach to hunt for a piece of sea glass. "We owe Carlos big time."

"I'll tell him you said that; he's my brother. In fact, Carlos is why I chose to move to Seahaven."

Jonathan stops in the middle of the sidewalk and faces me. "Whatever he said or did to get you to come here, I'm glad."

I'm startled at his words, but the moment is over as soon as it's begun. He's walking faster now, which is good because the sky has darkened into dusk. Moving quickly keeps us relatively warm. On our way to the beach, we come upon Carolina who has changed into gray sweats and a navy knit hat. She's jogging with the biggest dog I've ever seen, almost completely white. Carolina stops when she sees us and introduces Rocky. He's wearing a red and black vampire cape that is fastened under his belly. Jonathan quickly takes a few photos because one of the items on our list is "dog in a costume." Rocky seems completely oblivious to our good-natured laughter.

"Gotta keep moving!" she calls over her shoulder as she takes off again at a good clip, Rocky at her side. "See you at the party!"

We wave and hurry along. It's a tad difficult to find sea glass in the dark, although the moon is rising now, and icy pinpricks of stars are gleaming high above. "I have some sea glass at home," I say. "Why don't we run by my apartment so I can grab a piece?"

Jonathan checks his tablet again. "It has to be from the beach, sand included," he replies. We continue walking on the cold sand, heads bent. "Are you a collector?"

"I am now," I say cheerfully, as I tell him about the TNA group and Leah's bowl full of pretty glass. How the broken pieces become smooth again. How much like the grief journey it all is.

He nods, eyes focused on the ground. "Anna filled me in on all of that, of course. I have a few pieces of my own at home. It helped me when Mom died. Then there was the whole fiasco with Linnea," he adds with a grimace, pausing beside a large rock and poking around on the other side of it. "She didn't die, obviously, but it was a big loss anyway."

"Sure, I understand."

"All of my grandparents have died. I was close to my dad's father, Joe. That was a hard one. I was twenty-two, right out of college, starting my first teaching job. He was a teacher too. Middle school math. All his stories about working with the kids, about making a difference … He is the reason why I went into teaching."

"I'm sorry. He sounds like a wonderful man."

"He was."

There's nothing by these rocks so we keep walking. "Do you think we should go back now? We might not find any sea glass here in the dark."

He checks his tablet again. "We still have an hour, and no one else is down here searching, so let's stay a little longer. Unless you're too cold."

"No, I'm good." Actually, I'm freezing, but I like being out here with him like this. No lesson plans to talk about, no stage blocking or set designs to consider. Just the two of us. On a mission. I hope I can help him win.

We meander a little closer to the water when I finally spy a good-sized piece of clear glass shining in the moonlight. "I got one! Look!"

We squat in the sand and our hands touch as we both move eagerly to pick it up. I feel a little spark and I'm quite sure it's not static electricity. He quickly moves his hand away. "Go ahead, you take it. Get some of the sand too, so they know we took it from the beach."

As we make our way back to the Community Center, we stop by the Sea Star Candy Shop and add a cellophane-wrapped white chocolate sea star to our treasure bag. A few blocks later, I realize that we're holding hands. Despite the nip in the air, his hand is warm and mine feels just right in his.

"We need two more things," he says happily, swinging my hand. "The mask and the song."

"Right! It's going to be so warm inside! Do you think they'll have hot apple cider and something to eat? I can't wait to—"

An ambulance siren interrupts my hopeful chatter. Approaching the Center, we see a crowd of costumed people murmuring quietly on the lawn. The siren abruptly stops, and we all watch, stunned, as two EMTs rush to the back of the van and hustle a stretcher into the building.

Jonathan and I hurry to the edge of the crowd where I spy Jonathan's Aunt Anna from the TNA group. It's no surprise that she's dressed as a mermaid. Her silvery teal "scales" glisten under the artificial streetlights, and perched on top of her long yellow wig is an exquisite crown made entirely of shells and sea glass. I want to ask her about it, but my admiration will have to wait until another day.

"Anna, what's going on?" I ask, biting my lower lip.

"It's Kit Gilmore," she says, hugging herself with goose-pimpled arms. "They think she had another heart attack."

# Chapter 19

*Siren blaring,* the ambulance zips away from the Community Center with Marshall holding Kit's hand as he sits anxiously beside her on the stretcher. Tess and the children follow close behind with Luca in his silver truck. I turn to Jonathan, my voice trembling with anxiety. "You go ahead and finish the scavenger hunt without me, okay?" I hold out the little notebook and fabric bag. "I need to go to the hospital."

"I'm coming with you."

"No! I want you to win. You said—"

"I know I said it was important for me to win. I always want to win. But the scavenger hunt is just a game, and this is more important." He takes my notebook and bag and stuffs them into his larger treasure bag. "I'm going with you." His voice is adamant yet kind. As he places his hands on my arms, I feel a steady, reassuring warmth through both layers of my clothing, all the way down to my skin.

I look at the people who are streaming back into the Center, then at him. "Are you sure? You could go in there now, make the mask and write the song yourself. I'm sure the judges would make an exception … because of Aunt Kit. You could still win."

He leans in and whispers in my ear. "Elena, I *am* winning."

A tiny shiver of anticipation runs through me when I hear his words, but there's no time to process them now. I need to get to Kit.

Later—much later—that night, Jonathan and I head over to Waker's Beach where there's an all-night diner. It's four o'clock in the morning and we're both very hungry since the last thing we ate was the white chocolate sea star and a vending machine granola bar at the hospital. We both order a three-egg omelet: mine with cheddar, mushrooms, and onions; Jonathan's with Swiss cheese, sausage, and peppers—along with seasoned hash browns, crispy bacon, and grilled English muffins.

We're mostly silent as we scarf down the food. The place is empty except for a police officer sitting at the counter nursing a cup of coffee as he flirts with the lone waitress, and a teenage couple sitting on the same side of a booth, close together. Ryan and I always sat together like that when we were eating, close enough to touch. When Jonathan and I were shown to our booth, I sat down and patted the seat beside me. He saw me do this, then deliberately sat across from me. I was a little hurt at first because it seemed—through the excitement of the scavenger hunt and the bizarre night at the hospital—like we were getting closer, so I wondered why he didn't want to sit next to me. I think he saw the question in my eyes because he reached across the old ivory-flecked Formica tabletop and held my left hand in both of his. He must have noticed by now that I'm still wearing my wedding ring but it doesn't seem to bother him. "I'd like to sit across from you so I can see your face while we talk." He cleared his throat. "Is that okay?"

Is it okay? Yes, it is. So much more than okay. "I kind of like looking at your face too," I replied with a grin.

Now we're pushing away our plates and sipping our coffee. Caffeine at this hour might not be a good idea, but I have the feeling I'm not going to be sleeping any time soon, so I indulge in a cappuccino. I really don't want this night to end.

Jonathan must be a mind reader because after some small talk about who might have won the Scavenger Hunt, and the happy fact that Kit had passed out because of low blood sugar and not from another "heart event," he suggests that we drive over to Long Sands Beach in York to watch the sunrise.

"That's a great idea," I say with a delighted smile. A perfect ending to an almost-perfect day. Of course, it would have been more perfect if Aunt Kit hadn't been taken to the hospital, but other than that … "You know, I was talking to Tess and her daughter the other day. Eva. Did you meet her?"

"I saw them at the scavenger hunt and at the hospital, remember? They were dressed as Rory and Lorelai, aka the Gilmore Girls."

"Oh, that's right! Anyway, I was talking with her mother about the sunrise when Eva jumped in and reminded me that the sun isn't *rising*; it's the *Earth* that's moving. That's why Eva calls the sunrise an *Earth-move*."

Jonathan chuckles as he finishes his coffee and sets the mug down carefully. "That's clever, especially for an eleven-year-old, but I like the word sunrise better. More poetic." He adjusts his glasses and peers at the bill, then sets some money down.

"I agree. Here, let me pay for my half."

"It's on me. You can get it next time."

Next time. I like the sound of that.

We sit in Jonathan's car by Long Sands Beach until the first faint line of light appears on the horizon.

"You warm enough?" he asks as we exit the car. "I've got an extra pair of gloves in the trunk."

"I'm fine." After the hospital and before the diner, we each went back to our apartments and changed out of our Halloween costumes into warmer clothes. I clap my mittened hands together and pull my fleece-lined winter hat over my ears. "Are you okay?"

"Better than okay!" He takes my hand in his—mitten to glove—and we make our way down to the sand. The tide is going out now; stones and shells are scattered across the beach in the wake of high tide. Maybe we'll find more sea glass too.

We watch as the sky brightens … bit by bit, layer by layer. Another thin band of dusky orange light paints the sky, streaming through wispy clouds. A few bold streaks of scarlet wash on top of the orange. We hold the moment in silence. Together.

As we begin to walk, Jonathan tells me about growing up in Seahaven, his parents and siblings, his tenure at Seahaven High.

"Were you and Linnea high school sweethearts?"

"God, no. We met two years ago when she joined the staff fresh out of the University of Maine at Augusta."

The small waves make a faint shushing sound. "She's younger than you?"

"Eight years." He grimaces and we pause again, facing the water and the brightening sky. "It wasn't a big deal at first, and with some relationships it might not have been a problem at all, but … "

"Hey, I get it. My freshman year of college, before I met Marc, I dated someone who was twenty-seven. When you're that young, the age gap makes a difference."

"You're right. I wish I'd called it off."

"The wedding?"

"Yeah." He squeezes my hand and we meander north. Every time I look away from Jonathan and across the water, I see a different colored sky. "I should never have asked her to marry me," he finally says. "Looking back, I understand that hindsight really is 20/20. I can see that my mom's death had a lot to do with how I rushed into that relationship."

"That makes sense."

"Also, planning the wedding brought out the worst in her … in both of us."

"I remember planning my wedding to Marc." Usually when I think about this, there's a lump in my throat the size of a granny apple, but today I find I can easily keep going. "There was so much to do! His mom helped a lot, but Marc was supportive, and he made some of the big decisions with me."

"You were lucky."

"I was." Walking with him, sea salt air caressing my cold face, I almost say, *I am*.

"As much as it hurt at the time, I admire Linnea for having the courage to call it off."

"Although it would have been much better if she did it before you were standing at the altar."

"Probably," he replies with a chuckle.

"Now that would have taken real courage." I stop suddenly, let go of Jonathan's hand and crouch down. Taking off my left mitten with my teeth, I extend cold fingers into the newly-wet sand and scoop up several pieces of azure sea glass. "Look!" I'm grinning with excitement as I hold one of the pieces up to the light and pocket the others.

"Ah … treasures of the sea! And such a beautiful color." He stoops and picks up a smooth gray stone, perfectly round, with a creamy white line running across it. "Look, I found a treasure too." He traces his finger along the line on the stone and looks at me. "Linnea, Mom … all of that was then. And this is now."

I face him and meet his gaze. "Marc and Ryan … That was then. This is now."

He pockets the stone and puts his arm around me as we continue walking. "No more rushing into things."

"No more rushing," I agree.

We walk a bit more in silence before heading back to the car. The sun has rounded its way over the horizon now; it promises to be a blinding white ball of fire, so we angle ourselves away from it.

"I can see that the sea glass is important to you," Jonathan states. "Do you … " He hesitates and I sense that whatever he says next is going to shift our relationship into something more heartfelt. "Do you feel smoother now? I mean, after Marc's death and the move up here … after Ryan leaving. You've been through a lot."

I walk a little faster because I'm truly feeling the cold now, and because I want to think about my answer before I speak. His long legs catch up to me quickly. "I'm sorry, I didn't mean to—"

"It's okay," I reply as he unlocks the car and we climb in. With the heat blasting, I'm able to take off my hat and mittens. "I'm glad you asked," I say after a few minutes, finally settling into the warmth. "And thank you for waiting so patiently."

He reaches across the gear shift and lays his hand on top of my open palm, one piece of the blue sea glass clasped safely between our hands.

"I do feel smoother now," I say with a tender smile. "And there's something else I've been through that I want to share with you. I didn't just lose my husband two years ago. I also lost … Finn."

"Finn?" He frowns, as if I've added several pieces to a puzzle that he thought was complete.

"My baby. Marc's and mine. I miscarried two weeks after he died."

"Oh, Elena, I'm so sorry. What a terrible thing." He squeezes my hand, then takes the sea glass and runs his fingers around the smooth edges. "I wish I could have been there for you."

I smile as I move a bit closer and kiss him lightly on the lips. "What's important is that you're here for me now."

# Chapter 20

*The following Monday,* I head up to Jonathan's classroom before the students arrive. He's already at his desk, going over lesson plans for the day. The chalkboard is covered in lyrics from the musical *Hamilton*, and he's wearing a "Rise Up" baseball cap which looks a little incongruous with his blue plaid collared shirt and red tie. I'm surprised he isn't dressed like Tony Award-winning actor and director Lin-Manuel Miranda.

I knock lightly on the open door and he smiles when he sees me, then sets aside his notebook. "Elena! Good morning!"

"Good morning yourself! I wanted to say thank you again for the other night. I really appreciate—"

"It's no problem," he replies, standing up and joining me at the doorway. "I'm glad I was there for you."

"You were there for me at the hospital, and I had a good time with you before and after that too. Scavenger hunting and omelets and sunrises and so on." We smile at each other. "Since it's because of me that you didn't get to win this year, I got you this … " I pull a small box out of my tote bag and hand it to him.

"Oh, you didn't have to … " Jonathan's protests turn into hearty laughter as he opens the box and pulls out a gold plastic toy trophy, no bigger than a salt shaker. "I love it!" He jogs to his desk and places it on top of a stack of books. “It’s perfect! Thank you so much—”

Not realizing that I’ve followed him, he turns to head back to the door and collides right into me. I’m knocked off balance, but he catches me and suddenly he’s holding me tight and we’re staring at each other. I believe I’ve stopped breathing and maybe he has too. Neither one of us is letting go. His eyes are smiling at me as if to ask a question. I’m not sure what the question is but I’m pretty sure I want to say yes.

No questions get asked or answered because the bell for first period rings, startling us out of wherever we just were. Benjamin Cho and Kalila Jones—the *Our Town* stars—burst into the room at that moment, heading to their seats in the front row. Breaking apart immediately, Jonathan and I hear two loud gasps and a few giggles. Excited whispering breaks out as more students stream into the room.

I turn toward the door, but Jonathan catches my hand and whispers, “See you at rehearsal.” I’m trying to hide a delighted smile, but the kids are still whispering and giggling, so I just nod and rush back to my own classroom.

Rehearsal goes well. There are only a few short weeks until opening night, and everyone is already off-book because they’ve got their lines down cold. I don’t remember making such good progress at Dorchester High when I directed *You Can’t Take It with You* or *Almost, Maine,* but I’m not complaining!

Jonathan and his team have completed the *Our Town* set and it looks amazing. Ryan’s influence shows in the bright colors and some of the textural elements, especially in the graveyard scene. Rehearsals have already started for his new Broadway show and he won’t be coming back to Seahaven anytime soon, so I take some photos of the stage and the cast members, and text them to him with a note of gratitude.

Later that day when I get home from school, Jezebel sits on my lap as I'm reading my email. She keeps trying to sit on the keyboard and I keep pulling her off. I'm surprised to see a message from Vivian. I haven't heard from her since I gave her Finn's sonogram. Curious, I hold Jezebel against my chest and read.

*Dearest Elena,*

*I enjoyed our visit last month very much and want to thank you especially for the sonogram of baby Finn.*

*Even though my heart is broken that we never got to meet Finn or hold him in our arms, I feel blessed to have been introduced to him, by you, in this way.*

*Next Saturday, November 11, marks the second anniversary of the day we lost Marc. I'm hoping you'll be able to join me at the cemetery, at whatever time is convenient for you. I've been going there every few months just to say hello to him (I know it's silly, but maybe you understand) and on the one-year anniversary, I took special flowers and said a prayer.*

*I've finally sold the house and am heading to Florida on the fifteenth. I would love a chance to hug you one more time before I leave Massachusetts for good. You are the daughter that I didn't get to have in this lifetime, and I hope in some small way that I was like a mother to you.*

*Please let me know if and when you will meet me at Marc's grave.*

*Love,*
*Vivian*

There are tears in my eyes when I finish reading, and I kiss Jezebel gently on the head before placing her on the floor. I stand

and stretch, then twist the wedding ring on my finger. For the first time, it feels like it's in the way. Maybe even unnecessary.

November 11 is also opening night for *Our Town*, but I don't have to be at school until four o'clock that day. I notice a few anxious butterflies in my stomach as I consider standing with Vivian at Marc's grave, but I would like to see her before she moves to Florida. I can drive to Lexington, meet Vivian at the cemetery, and still be back here in plenty of time for our first performance.

I quickly email her an affirmative reply, then head to the kitchen to get ready for Kit who is joining me for supper.

"You seem to have settled in quite nicely," Kit says on arrival, handing me a pretty fall bouquet as she looks around my apartment. "I like what you've done with this space." Jezebel jumps off the sofa and winds her way around Kit's legs. "Look at this little beauty!" She picks Jez up and nuzzles her furry head.

"Yes, Jezebel is an excellent companion," I reply as I take Kit's heavy cardigan and hang it on the wrought iron coat rack by the front door, then head to the kitchen in search of a vase. "And I actually like it here, although I had my doubts at first."

"Just for the record, there was never any doubt in *my* mind." Kit heads to the stove and lifts the lid on a large pot. "This smells delicious. I didn't know you were such a good cook!"

"I do okay with my mom's recipes," I say, hiding a smile. "I'm out of practice, but it does smell good, so I think I did everything right. It's Pollo Guisado, a special chicken stew with a magical combination of adobo, sofrito, and some other spices. It was Mom and Dad's favorite. I think you'll love it."

"I have no idea what any of that is, but I'm happy to make your mother's acquaintance through her food." She wanders through the kitchen and back to the living room, then settles in the rocking chair. Jezebel follows and makes herself at home on Kit's lap, immediately shedding black fur all over Kit's immaculate cream-colored gauze pants. "I never thought about getting a cat, or even a dog for that matter. We didn't have one in Brunswick, and it was impossible to think about when I was traveling so much. Once I retired from modeling and got settled in my cottage, it never even crossed my mind." She strokes Jez's back, and I can hear her loud throaty purrs even though I'm in the next room, chopping carrots to go with the Guisado.

"Maybe it's time for you to get a cat," I call, smiling at the thought of Kit with a feline companion. "There's an animal shelter in Wells, I think."

"Ollie's mom was allergic, so they didn't have pets either, but we talked about getting two dogs and two cats," she mused, slowly rocking back and forth.

"You could ask Dr. Brightman about the best place to adopt," I suggest.

"Good idea. Has Jezebel met our town vet yet?"

I add the carrots to the pot of stew and clink the lid back on, then take a seat on the sofa. "She sure has. Got her shots soon after I got to Seahaven along with a thorough exam. Dr. B. was so gentle with Jezebel; she started purring as soon as he picked her up from the carrier!"

"I've heard good things about him." Jezebel jumps off Kit's lap and wanders to her water bowl in the kitchen doorway. We sit in companionable silence for a few minutes, savoring the spicy scent of the stew and letting the soothing music of Liquid Mind drift around us. "Oh, I know what I wanted to ask!" Kit suddenly exclaims. "Have you heard from Ryan?"

"He's got the lead in a new musical by Lin-Manuel Miranda that's heading to Broadway in the spring."

"Ah, I knew that boy was something special. He'll go far, I think." Kit stands and stretches, reaching her fingertips toward the ceiling.

I stand with her and nod. "I'm sure you're right. And I'm glad our paths crossed when they did. He gave me … He brought me back to myself."

"And now … Jonathan?" she smiles mischievously as we head back to the kitchen.

"What about him?" I ask, although I know what's coming next.

"I saw the two of you together at the scavenger hunt. And the word is that he came with you to the hospital after my last unfortunate incident."

"Would you like some wine?" I'm avoiding her question but am pleased that she asked.

"I would love some wine. Can I do anything to help?"

I busy myself getting two wine glasses from the cupboard and uncorking a bottle of Riesling. "Thank you, but everything's done." I fill a glass and hand it to her as she settles into one of my kitchen chairs. "I'm waiting for the carrots to simmer a bit longer. The table is set and the bread is in the basket." Leaning against the counter by the sink, I take a long swallow of wine.

After a brief pause, Kit clears her throat and asks me about Jonathan again.

"I like him," I finally say. "A lot. We're in the getting-to-know-you stage right now. I don't know what will happen next."

"That's exactly as it should be," Kit replies, joining me at the sink and clinking her glass with mine. "Relationships can be quite a mystery."

"Now that's a philosophical statement if I ever heard one!" I set down my wine glass and take the lid off the Guisado, stirring gently and testing one of the carrot coins. Not soft enough. "What about you and Marshall Sorenson? Is that relationship a mystery too?"

Kit laughs heartily and sits back down at the table, gazing out the window at the heavy November sky with a slight smile on her face. "You know, it *is* a mystery to me that this wonderful man, whom I have known for more than forty years—first in a professional capacity and then as a friend—could now be my lover and lifelong companion."

"Could be?" I arch an eyebrow expectantly as I sit across from her at the table. The watery afternoon light is slowing fading into dusk and I turn on the small lamp next to me. It casts a soft glow over us. "Or is?"

She smiles and takes another sip of wine. "Could be. Very possibly might be. He's officially retiring at the end of the year and is looking to buy a house up here permanently, as soon as he sells his condo in New York."

"Is that something you want too?" I'm curious about this woman whose losses have somehow made her more vibrant and giving instead of crushing her spirit.

"Oh, most definitely," she replies. I smile at the certainty in her voice. "He has been there for me, in so many ways, ever since he took me on as a client forty-some years ago. First as my agent, then as a guide through the strange waters of my new modeling career. After a while, whenever I was in New York in between gigs, I stayed with him and Cassie at their Park Avenue home. They were a second family to me after my dad died. My second family—Lillian, Olivia, Julia, Violet, Marshall, and Cassie."

"I'm glad you had a second family after Ollie died. As for Marshall, that is quite a long relationship," I comment as I head back to the stove to ladle out our dinner. "You've known him longer than I've been alive."

"An interesting way to look at it, I suppose. One thing's for sure … I don't want to give up my cottage. I've made it my home and I like being near Tess and Eva, even though after the wedding they'll be moving in with Luca and Teo. I've told Marshall that we can still be in a committed relationship even if we live in separate houses."

"Amen to that!" I set a bowl of Guisado in front of her and she breathes in the savory steam. "Here's to good food and good friends." I lift my wine glass to hers again in another toast.

"And here's to the mystery inherent in all relationships," Kit adds with a playful wink.

# Chapter 21

*Standing on the* faded brown grass at Marc's grave, I shiver in the crisp November air and stare at the two stones in front of me, hardly able to believe what I'm seeing. Vivian isn't here yet, or I would be hugging her fiercely right now.

Tears fill my eyes as I lay a bouquet of red roses in front of Marc's stone. Two years ago, when Vivian asked me what I wanted inscribed on it, I couldn't even begin to imagine an answer. But she has done well.

Marc Christopher Jeffries
1993 - 2021
Beloved son, husband, father
Life Is Not Forever. Love Is.

I gasp at the word *father*. She must have had to pay the engraver to come out here and add it after I told her about Finn. What a generous and loving thing to do.

But the thing that really brings tears to my eyes right now is the smaller stone, made of the same silver-flecked granite, resting about a foot in front of Marc's. It brings me to my knees—literally—in the damp freshly-dug dirt.

Finn Christopher Jeffries
2021
Beloved son & grandson
You are greatly loved.

I am touching Finn's stone with my bare hands when I hear footsteps. Vivian crouches beside me and puts her arm around my shoulder. We don't say a word. It's just the four of us here. One last time. My husband, who will always be my husband. My son, who will always be my son. My mother-in-law who is also a friend. And me. A family that will always be my family, even if life leads me to create a new family.

Eventually, I stand, brushing soil from my black slacks. Vivian turns to me. She's wearing a long navy winter coat with a hand-knit red scarf tucked around her neck. Her graying blond hair is brushed back from her high forehead and her eyes search mine. "Are you okay with what I've done here?" she asks. "I wasn't sure—"

"Vivian, I am so much more than okay. This is … perfect. Thank you." I pull her to me in a grateful hug and can feel her gloved hands trembling against my back. I know how hard this must be for her.

"After you gave me Finn's sonogram, I knew I had to change this," she says, finally pulling away from me to wipe her eyes with a tissue from her coat pocket. She is smiling now, looking at the two stones—one large, one small.

"I'm glad. And I'm sorry that I didn't come here with you after Marc died." There is some residue of guilt still clinging to me about this.

"Hush, dear girl," Vivian says softly, laying one hand on my arm and the other on Marc's stone. "I understand. You were taking care of yourself and that is how it should have been."

"But you had to do all of this … " I gesture to the gravestones. "… by yourself."

She pats both stones a few times, then straightens. "I wasn't alone. A few friends were with me through the hardest times at the beginning. My sister flew up from Florida and stayed several months. She helped me contact the cemetery."

"Still, I wish I'd been stronger … for both of us."

She shakes her head, making a *tsk-tsk* sound. "We're as strong as we need to be at any given time, Elena. If I hadn't been there, you would have found the strength to do what you needed to do."

I tip my head to the side, thinking about this.

"Look at how strong you are now. A person has to be strong to share their grief with a therapist, and to start all over again in a new school, a new town—meeting new colleagues and making friends." She takes hold of my forearms and peers at me inquisitively. "Yes?"

Can I admit how strong I am, how much strength it took to sit down in Camille's office that first time, and every time thereafter? How I didn't think I had it in me to move to Seahaven and begin a new life? I lay my cold, bare hands on hers and gaze back at her. "Yes," I finally admit.

"Very good," she says, nodding to herself in satisfaction, as if getting me to admit how strong I am was her ultimate goal today. She rubs her hands together, even though they must already be warm in those fur-lined leather gloves. "I'm going to my car now to get some flowers."

Later, I watch as Vivian lays her flowers next to mine. We stand with our arms around each other's waists in companionable silence. She says a brief prayer and we bow our heads. I feel a familiar sorrow in my heart, but it isn't leaden and weighted down like it used to be. Now the sorrow is more like a piece of glass that once was broken but has been smoothed and lightened by the rough waves of the ocean. It's easier to observe, to hold, to touch.

"I'm going to leave now," she says. "But first I want to ask you something. I wasn't sure if it was okay to ask, but my sister told me I should, so I'm going to do it. Because it might be important."

"Okay," I respond, drawing out the word cautiously.

"Is there someone … special … in your life now?" Her face is flushed but I can't tell if it's because of the question or because of the almost-winter chill in the air.

"Someone special?" I think I know where she's going with this and attempt to suppress a smile.

"You know," she says, bumping my elbow with hers conspiratorially. "A gentleman friend who might be … more than a friend?"

I feel my face heat up quickly despite the frigid November air.

"It's okay, Elena. Truly. If you've met someone in Seahaven, don't hesitate to let him into your life." She touches her hand to her heart and then to mine, resting it lightly on my coat. "It's time for you to be happy again. I want that for you. Marc and Finn would want that for you."

Her words reverberate through my entire being. I think about Ryan, and how perfect it was that I met him exactly when I did. Without even knowing he was doing it, just by being himself, he showed me the way back to myself. He was safe because I knew he wasn't going to stay. He showed me how to have fun again, that it was okay to laugh, to take pleasure in life where I'd been shut down for so long. I also think of Jonathan, who I pushed away at first because I didn't think I was strong enough to try a long-lasting relationship again. But my days of looking back with regret are over now. I know who I am—a strong woman with a whole lifetime of love and laughter ahead of me. And yes, I know … sorrow also.

I hug Vivian again and whisper in her ear, "His name is Jonathan. He's a history teacher at Seahaven High. But we're not … I mean, we haven't … "

Vivian bounces on her toes like a giddy teenager and claps her hands which make a muffled sound in the silent cemetery. "I understand, dear. You have my blessing." She gestures to the two gravestones which stand solidly rooted into the earth as they always will be. "And theirs." She blows me a kiss and heads down the narrow path to her car.

As she drives away, I reach into my coat pocket and pull out the piece of notebook paper where I'd written an additional "Goodbye Soliloquy" after rehearsal last week. Unfolding it carefully, I take a deep breath and read it aloud, occasionally glancing up at what remains of my Marc, my Finn.

"Marc, two years have gone by. You're not with us anymore. I sold our house. I moved to Seahaven and am teaching English there. Carlos lives nearby and he's in love with a great guy named Jasper. You would like him. I've been seeing a therapist named Camille, and I have a black cat named Jezebel. It's been hard living my life without you these last two years. And now I'm here saying good-bye. Not to you, Marc, but to the life and the love we shared.

"So … goodbye sweet little house in Dorchester. Goodbye to sleeping late on Sunday mornings, your cold feet in bed at night, your off-key singing, and the messy bathroom sink. The Sunday night dinners with your mom, reading together on our porch, and sitting side by side during Broadway shows in Boston. Goodbye to your hugs and kisses and silly jokes and your quiet way of letting me know that everything was always going to be all right. I loved you. I love you now. I will always love you.

"Dear Finn. Know that you were created from love. I wish with all my heart that you had been ready to be born … " My eyes cloud over with tears, so I simply stand there several minutes longer, breathing in the crisp autumn air, breathing deeply into this welcome sense of gratitude and release that I'm feeling.

Before I leave, I kiss two pieces of white sea glass and lay one on each of the gravestones. I wiggle the wedding ring from my finger and lay it on Marc's stone along with the paper bearing my soliloquy.

I don't wave goodbye.

I don't say another goodbye as I turn to leave.

Because I know that they will both always be with me. My first family.

On the way home, I stop at Whole Foods to buy flowers, chocolates, and balloons for the *Our Town* cast. I hum along to Jason Mraz's upbeat, toe-tapping song "Have It All." My heart feels lighter than it has in a long time. I pull up in front of Seahaven High at four-fifteen, knowing that the others are probably wondering where I am, but I sit in my car a few more minutes, cherishing this lightness of being, this absence of deep sorrow, smiling to myself because of what Vivian had said and done.

I want to catch Time and hold it still. I'd like to hang onto this moment forever, savoring the tense expectancy of opening night jitters along with the joy and excitement that are careening around inside of me. It is live theatre after all; as prepared as all the cast members are, who knows what might happen? As interested as Jonathan and I are in each other, who knows what the future will bring?

But Time, as usual, marches on. Taking a deep breath, I eagerly get out of the car, fill my arms with what I've bought, and head toward the school's side entrance.

The students, the stage, our first audience … and Jonathan… are waiting for me.

# Please Stay in Touch!

I hope that *Sea Glass Memories* touched your heart and soul in some way. If it was meaningful for you, please help me share this book with others by leaving a short review on Amazon here.

You might like to sign up for my (colorful, not-too-long) free monthly author newsletter, Stories That Stir Heart & Soul. You'll be the first to read about:

- my monthly give-aways of recommended heart & soul-stirring paperback novels (sometimes my own, but not always)
- contests with nifty prizes
- recipes
- background info about some of the characters
- information about upcoming novels from the wild wanderings of my imagination
- and lots more!

**I'd love to hear from you about how Elena and Aunt Kit's stories of loss and renewal touched your heart and soul!**

Website: AnneMarieBennett.com
Email: AnneMarie@AnneMarieBennett.com
Social Media: facebook.com/annemariebennettauthor
Social Media: instagram.com/annemariebennett520/

# A Note from the Author About Sea Glass & Grief

Since I was a teenager, I've created a writer's habit of collecting interesting tidbits from magazines and places online (images and articles, news clippings, etc.) that I "might use in a book someday."

As I was stirring my imagination to create Elena's and Kit's stories for *Sea Glass Memories*, I went through my (rather large) box of these interesting tidbits. My heart lit up with recognition when I came across a yellowed page from *Yankee Magazine*. It contained a 1986 essay called "Collecting Mermaid's Tears" by Tim Clark. You can read it here if you like. His words inspired me to use the metaphor of sea glass as a means of for Elana and others to process the grief they are experiencing. It also gave me a way to connect with Anna M. French, the children's author. You'll read more about Anna (along with Leah and Dr. Brightman) in Seahaven Sunrise Book 3, *Wish Upon a Sea Star,* coming in December 2024.

Three other articles found online helped me to make sense of and shape this metaphor for the novel. They are:

Grief is Like Sea Glass, by Lorelei Bonet
The Edge of Grief, by Ellen Frankel LCSW
From Shard to Sea: The Evolution of Grief, by Liz Petrone

I am deeply indebted to these authors who have experienced their own grief journeys and taken the time to gift us with their wisdom. I hope that their stories are meaningful for you as well.

A few books about loss and grief also helped me both personally and professionally as I was telling Elena and Kit's stories:

*How to Carry What Can't Be Fixed*, by Megan Devine
*The Wild Edge of Sorrow*, by Francis Weller
*Unattended Sorrow*, by Stephen Levine

# Gratitudes

**Jeff, My Husband-** We have experienced grief together and apart. I know of no better comfort than to be held in your arms when I feel sorrow in my heart, and to offer you the same. Thank you for holding my hand through the last thirty-two years together, and for supporting my "writing habit," always, no questions asked.

**My Beta Readers-** You know who you are, but I'm going to name you here anyway. Your eager responses, suggestions, ideas, and corrections made a world of difference in the polish and shine that blesses this book's pages. I am grateful for Marti Beddoe, Pam Papworth, Taylor Williams, and Carolyn Dumaine.

**"Last Eyes" Readers-** A special thank you to Margaret Banks in Australia and Stacy Green in Kentucky, for being my "last eyes" before I sent the manuscript to my book designer. You didn't bat an eye when I told you I had a three-day deadline, and that means the world to me.

**Writing Teachers-** I will forever be thankful for **Jennifer Louden** whose online class I stumbled into in 2016. Her teachings about small steps, celebration, persistence, and motivation changed my life as a writer. Also, **Jessica Brody**, whose *Save the Cat Writes a*

*Novel* book and online courses are helping to shape my fiction in a myriad of ways that continue to surprise and delight me.

**Writing Community**- My gratitude continues for all the direction, support, and kindness I've received from the Women's Fiction Writers Association (WFWA). I have learned so much from all of you and hope to be able to give back as much as I've received.

**My Book Designer,** Kozakura. I feel blessed to have found you on Fiverr.com in 2019 when I was getting ready to publish my first novel, and grateful that you've been available to me ever since. The compassion, care, and attention to detail that you put into creating a beautiful interior design makes my heart very happy.

**My Cover Designer, Lynn Andreozzi**- What a treasure I discovered on Reedsy.com last year! I appreciate your listening ear and your guidance as we created this beautiful cover together.

**Author Kazuo Ishiguru**- The quote of yours that I share in Chapter 16 made a huge impact on my own life's journey, and I thank you for allowing me to share it in *Sea Glass Memories* through the eyes of Elena's grief journey, and Kit's story as well.

**The Towns of Wells and Ogunquit, Maine**- Over the last five years, I've secluded myself in various spots in your lovely seaside towns, in order to give myself over to the stories in my novels that want to be told. I am grateful to the staff at The Falls in Ogunquit and Garnsey Brothers Realty in Wells for fabulous accommodations, beautiful views, and excellent customer service. You make my writer's heart happy!

# Book Club Discussion / Journaling Prompts

1. Which character do you identify with the most? Why?

2. Was there a time in your life when you had to decide to leave a beloved home and start over somewhere new? What prompted you to make that decision? How did it turn out?

3. Rent the DVD or stream the movie *Our Town*. What wisdom do you see or hear that might help you or someone you love who is grieving?

4. Re-read the quote from author Kazuo Ishiguro in Chapter 16. Do his words resonate with you? What is the "other life" you might have had? How can you reconcile the life you are having now with what you thought your life would be?

5. Leah St. James, the social worker who leads the support group *Together Not Alone*, collects sea glass and uses it as a touchstone for her own grief journey. Have you ever used a physical object as a touchstone to help you through a difficult time? What was it and how did it help you?

6. Elena experienced a double loss in a very short period of time. Do you think that made her grief journey more difficult than Kit's loss? Or is it important not to measure and compare?

7. Write a poem or song, or create a collage that gives expression to a current or previous loss.

8. Elena's brother Carlos helped her immensely after the loss of her husband and child. Lillian was a lifeline for Kit after Ollie died. In thinking about a recent loss of your own, who was there to support you and how did they help? Did anyone surprising step forward to help you carry your grief? Did anyone disappoint you by stepping away from you during your grief journey?

9. Sunrise is another important theme in this book. When was the last time you experienced a sunrise? What was it like?

10. Ollie's mom, Lillian, tells Kit that when grieving, it helps to carry that person's light into the world. Is there someone no longer with us who lit up *your* life? How can you carry their light forward?

11. A. Powell Davies said that "those whom we love … can never leave us." Do you believe that this is true? What do these words mean to you? What did these words mean to Kit, Elena, Jonathan, and Anna in this novel?

# Additional Books by Anne Marie Bennett

## FICTION

Come As You Are (Young Adult)
My Other Dad (Middle Grades)
All You Need is Love … and Lilacs (Novella)
Dragonflies at Night: More Than a Love Story (Women's Fiction)
Feathers in the Sand (Seahaven Sunrise #1)

## NONFICTION

Bright Side of the Road: A Spiritual Journey Through Breast Cancer
Sunflower Spirit Workbook for Women with Cancer
Through the Eyes of SoulCollage®
Into the Heart of SoulCollage®
Walking the Path of SoulCollage®
Magical Inner Journeys: 44 Guided Imagery Scripts

*Those whom we love do indeed leave us,*
*and when we lose them no spoken words can lessen our grief.*

*But what they were can never leave us.*
*The strength of their presence,*
*the gentleness of their sympathy,*
*the warmth of their love-*
*these are ours always,*
*interfused with our thought and blended with our lives.*

**~ A. Powell Davies**

Made in United States
North Haven, CT
16 November 2024

60397443R00124